QUEST
FOR
LIBERTY

Quest for Liberty

Robert H. Rowe

Peter E. Randall
Publisher
Portsmouth, New Hampshire
2001

© 2001 by Robert H. Rowe
Printed in the United States of America

Peter E. Randall Publisher
Box 4726, Portsmouth, NH 03802

Distributed by University Press of New England
Hanover and London

Photo page 36: Boston in 1775, from *Paul Revere's Ride* by David Hackett Fischer, © 1995 by David Hackett Fischer. Used with permission of Oxford Unversity Press, Inc.

Library of Congress Cataloging-in-Publication Data

Rowe, Robert H., 1932
   Quest for Liberty / Robert H. Rowe
     p. cm.
   Includes bibliographical references.
   ISBN 0-914339-92-3 (alk. paper)
     1. New Hampshire--History--Revolution, 1775-1783--Fiction.
   2. United States--History--Revolution, 1775-1783--Fiction.
   3. Amherst (N.H.)--Fiction. 4. Pacifists--Fiction. I. Title
   PSA3568.093 Q47 2001
   813'.6--dc21

                                                            00-66495

Acknowledgments

I would like to express my appreciation to the many individuals who assisted in the research and writing of *Quest for Liberty* over the past five years.

First and foremost, my profound thanks to my wife, Helen. She was there offering courteous suggestions and editing as chapter after chapter was drafted. Certainly without her encouragement the book would have ended at the idea stage.

The professional assistance offered by Geoffrey Douglas in structuring and editing the book was of the greatest value.

William Overholt was most generous with his time and computer in drawing the maps, sophisticated task that was far beyond my abilities.

Last but not least I am grateful to the staff of the Amherst Library and the New Hampshire State Library in providing research assistance which included many nineteenth century books and documents that allowed me to provide accuracy and life to the local characters. Especially helpful were the early biographies of New Hampshire citizens that were written by Charles Atherton. Without this source, characters such as Joshua Atherton, Thompson Maxwell, and Wyseman Claggett would have been left to the imagination of the author.

Robert H. Rowe

Author's Note

Quest for Liberty is fiction but, with few exceptions, the characters and events are fact and have been verified through 19th-century historical documents. Minor characters and dialogue are the product of the author's imagination and literary license, solely to add the life and drama so often lacking in academic journals. Protagonists Joshua Atherton, Loyalist and lawyer, and Thompson Maxwell, Whig and warrior, did live in Amherst, New Hampshire, and did take part in the activities described in the book. Also fact, but one seldom noted, is that on December 14, 1774, four months before Concord and Lexington, members of the New Hampshire militia attacked Fort William and Mary in New Castle, at the mouth of Portsmouth Harbor, and in January 1776, six months before the signing of the Declaration of Independence, the first New Hampshire constitution was adopted. My goal in this book is to describe in a historical novel format the activities of these two remarkable men and the events that occurred in New Hampshire at the start of the Revolutionary War.

The bibliography in the back of this book lists a few of the documents utilized as source materials. Unfortunately, few are available except through antiquarian book dealers, historical societies, or state libraries.

The site for most of the events, Amherst Village, is one of those few New England towns that have retained their colonial charm; it remains much as it was at the beginning of the American Revolution. With the smallest leap of imagination, the visitor to Amherst can be transformed back in time more than two hundred years. You can sit on the common where the militia mustered for their march to Massachusetts on April 21, 1775, and view the Second Meetinghouse and many of the homes described in the book. You need only transform in your mind's eye the paved streets to dirt, the cars to horses and wagons, and the dogs to livestock, and the stage will be set for *Quest for Liberty.*

Robert H. Rowe

1

JOSHUA ATHERTON

IT HAD BEEN TWO DAYS since his last meal. He wondered, barely caring, if he still had the strength to rise. The straw covering his cot was damp with sweat, its legacy of prisoners—many, he knew, now dead. Of the twelve men he shared the cell with, all but two—himself and the only man he guessed to be older—were huddled forlornly in the center, in the four-foot square of pale sunlight that entered through the only window, which was too far above to see out. He wondered dimly if the day was cloudless, if New Hampshire's October colors were bright or dull this year, if the first frost would come soon. Then, too weak to sustain his wondering, he gave himself up to sleep.

In the dream that came, he saw his wife, Abigail, standing in front of their home against a backdrop of snow. In her eyes was the mix of pleading and patience he had come to know so well. And then she spoke—"Please, Joshua, don't"—and the hurt deepened, then swelled to tears that dropped to the snow at her feet. And then he was holding her, his face buried in her hair, holding her and rocking her, and swearing for the thousandth time that he would not fail her again.

It was a dream he had often. The dream of his failure as husband, lawyer, patriot, Christian, and lover of peace. Lover of peace—that was his *biggest* failure, the root of his undoing. He dreamed often, and prayed continually: that he be given the chance to make it right, that he be returned somehow to the life of freedom he had known, that he be granted the chance to unravel the awful knot he had made of a peaceful, prosperous life.

Yet what would he do differently? What *could* he do differently? It was on this question that he always stumbled, that his prison reveries came up short. He was, he knew, a good man, a lover of God and country and family, a man who would not willingly do harm to any creature on earth. Yet he was a Tory: His allegiance, if not his sympathies, remained with George III. And when it came to matters of conscience, Joshua Atherton was not a man to give ground.

So here he would remain, in the county prison of Exeter, New Hampshire, to which he had arrived, condemned by his fellows, bundled like produce in the back of a tumbril. And from which he was likely to leave—as had so many of his fellows already—in a box.

"Abigail, I'm so sorry. Please forgive me." He said the words aloud, seeing in his mind the face of his wife, weeping silently, stoically, the morning they took him away.

"Can you not hold your tongue, Joshua? Can you not keep your own counsel? Can you not see the peril you create?" She pleaded with him—twenty times, thirty, a hundred, sometimes naming the names of other men they knew, other Tories, who kept their sympathies to themselves—until the very morning they had come for him. And he had answered the same way every time: "An honest man must speak his conscience, Abigail. There is no value to freedom without the freedom to speak."

And in the end, on the rainy morning they had arrived with their muskets and their tumbril to take him from his home in Amherst, over muddy roads to Exeter, more than thirty miles away, his wife had stood quietly and wept. And even after that, on the days she visited, with her brave smiles and her baskets of knitted socks and homemade bread, she made no mention of his folly, no reminders of her earlier advice. "Have courage, Joshua. Have faith and courage, and keep yourself strong"—this was the only advice she'd allowed herself since the day she'd watched him go.

It had been weeks, though, since she had even that to give. The roads between Amherst and Exeter, never better than furrowed sloughs of mud and hay, were impassable with the late-summer rains; soon snow would make the wagon trip too perilous to risk. Joshua, knowing he was relinquishing his last, best hope for strength or comfort, had written his wife that he would see her in the spring.

He doubted the truth of this. He doubted that he would see her ever again. He imagined her getting word of his passing through the governor's messenger, who would arrive at their home in Amherst with a letter conveying the "sympathies" of the crown. The thought filled him with dread. Not for himself—for he was unafraid of death—but for the prospect of Abigail, the mother of their three children, left without resources in a world whose cruelty she had yet to comprehend.

He coughed, then sat upright on his cot. Weakness overtook him; the effort was almost too much. He coughed once more, weakly, then placed his hand on the wall at his back. He would stand; he would walk to the light with the others. He would eat what gruel they gave him. For Abigail, only for Abigail, he would do his best to live.

THOMPSON MAXWELL

He had been fortunate, more fortunate than most. On the march to Isle au Noire, forty miles north of Montreal, the smallpox had stricken nearly a quarter of the troops. Of the two thousand men on the march, more than a tenth had died outright; hundreds more, Lieutenant Maxwell knew, would be dead before winter was out.

The cold was mounting. Now, in the fort at Ticonderoga, which the colonists had wrested from the British in May 1775, General Sullivan had ordered scouts to the nearest friendly communities to secure more blankets before the next frost. The scouts had yet to return. The nights were cruelly cold.

It had been a hard year, hard but well fought. In March, the British had abandoned Boston. Thompson Maxwell, with a company under his command, arrived in the city in time to see the last of the king's soldiers depart across the Charles. Then it had been on to New Haven, then Providence, and finally New York, where six thousand troops, under Gen. George Washington, had lost the Battle of Long Island only two months before.

But the tide of the war would soon turn. Barely three months from now, the Continental forces, again under General Washington, would achieve victories at Trenton and Princeton in New Jersey before losing the battle of Brandywine, then defeating General Burgoyne at Saratoga in what many later would say was the decisive battle of the war.

Thompson Maxwell was a part of much of this. And of much that had preceded it. A career soldier, he'd enlisted in a company of Rangers in 1757—he was not yet sixteen—and fought a dozen or more campaigns, many of them costly and savage, in the French and Indian War. He'd married after that, fathered five children, and made his living briefly as a farmer and hauler of freight between Amherst and Boston before arming himself once again following the dumping of tea in Boston Harbor in December 1773.

He was a Whig. Along with Sam Adams, John Hancock, and others who would risk their careers and lives in defying the British over the course of the next seven years, he believed fervently, passionately, that the colonies must be sovereign from the crown. And that the Tories who opposed this view were no better than the British themselves.

Now, shivering in his bedroll in a small sleeping cranny in the bowels of the fort at Ticonderoga, he thought about the winter to come. His men were tired; since the last of May, they had marched more than eight hundred miles in all and had done battle with the British at Trois-Rivières, Montreal, Jesus Isle, St. John's, and Isle au Noire. More than fifty of his command were dead, by either smallpox or musket wounds. Several dozen more were too weak or sick to march.

Yet march they would: tomorrow to Albany, where they would engage a band of Hessians for control of the fort at Troy; from there south to Delaware; then on to join General Washington outside Trenton in the fight with General Howe.

It would be a hard winter. There would be more losses, more sickness, and more death. Christmas, he knew, would take place once again without Sybel. It had been three years since he had shared a Christmas with his wife.

He thought of her now, as he often did in the minutes before he slept: asleep herself in their bed at home in Amherst, the mother of his children, forty years old last month. He was torn by guilt. So much of his life had been away from Amherst, putting the home obligations solely on her shoulders. She deserved better than being the wife of a soldier. Next year, he told himself, he would be home for her birthday. If the war was ended by then. If the promise was his to keep.

Amherst Meetinghouse
When the first meetinghouse, located at the corner of Mack Hill and Jones Road, was judged to be too small, a larger structure was constructed on the town common. In 1836 the building was moved from the common to the current location.

2

AMHERST
AUGUST 1773

JOSHUA STOOD NEXT TO HIS WIFE in front of Robert Means's store at the edge of the common, surveying the mass of humanity that surrounded him—carriages, wagons, horses and riders, men and women arriving on foot. Tomorrow, he thought, the village would be itself again: Cattle would once more be grazing on the common, the wagons and people would long since have scattered, sheep and chickens would be picking about in the yards. It would be as it had been yesterday, as it was every day but today. A child's crying or the restless baying of a hound would be all there was to break the quiet. But that was unthinkable now.

The crowds had been arriving since dawn. Benches had been placed and tables set; fires were already crackling, and stores of meat awaited the heated coals. At the far end of the common, on an expanse as large around as several house sites, four immense pine wall sidings lay flat on the ground. These were the walls of Amherst's new meetinghouse, whose frame would be raised by the villagers this day. It was the occasion for the large gathering: a joyous, prideful venture, the raising of the building that would symbolize the strength and unity of the town.

What a glorious day, thought Joshua. What a marvelous day to be alive. The sun was just rising above the trees; it would be clear and warm. From the far side of the common, he heard the trumpetlike voice of the aptly named Deacon Barker, chosen by the selectmen as master builder: "Are we all present? All accounted for?" he bellowed. "Remember, remember, thirty men to a side!"

He squeezed his wife's shoulder, "We're a fortunate family," he said.

She looked up at him and smiled.

They were indeed fortunate, even blessed. Joshua, already a respected lawyer with a growing practice, had just been appointed by the king himself, following Governor Wentworth's recommendation, as registrar of probate for the new county of Hillsborough, with Amherst as the county seat. Only months before he had moved his family and practice here; every sign pointed to the wisdom of this decision.

Amherst, in the two years since being named county seat, had grown and prospered almost beyond imagining. Already the largest and most active town in inland New Hampshire—only Portsmouth and Exeter were more prosperous—it was now enjoying a wave of new construction: homes, stores, county buildings, the county jail, and now this meetinghouse. The village's future, and that of its residents, seemed assured.

Joshua looked up to find Robert Means standing at his side. Means, perhaps the most well-to-do merchant in town, was, with his wife Mary, among the many neighbors he and Abigail counted as friends.

To the casual observer, the two men seemed in stark contrast. At a distance, Robert Means had a presence about him, almost of nobility—well over six feet tall and thin, somewhat emaciated, with a long, slender face and a straight, severe mouth. His plain but well-tailored long coat and waistcoat gave his appearance additional height. Means exuded prosperity and aloofness. Atherton, a foot shorter, could be easily overlooked in any crowd. His only distinguishing features were a rather prominent nose, his receding hair, and his girth; he looked like one who delighted in partaking of well-cooked meals. It was on drawing closer that Atherton stood out—his sparkling gray eyes, bright smile, and magnetic personality radiated the fact that he liked people. His quick mind enabled him to remember the smallest personal details; as a result, people trusted and felt a kinship with Atherton.

Together Atherton and Means watched as a dense thicket of men, somewhere between fifty and a hundred, formed a circle around Deacon Barker at the far side of the square.

"Surely this will be the finest meetinghouse in New Hampshire!" Means said, clapping Joshua on the back. "An apt rival to the Old South in Boston—people will see our steeple from afar, and will no longer dispute what our little village has become."

Joshua was fond of Robert Means. He enjoyed his high spirits, and knew him to be a man of goodwill. Still, he thought now, as the proprietor of a store whose doors faced the new building, his own prospects for growth could not be far from his mind.

The merchant seemed to read his thoughts. "And the commerce it will bring," he went on. "Just imagine all the commerce."

He paused briefly, then continued, his tone more thoughtful. "Joshua, Abigail"—he looked from one to the other. "It's not too late, you know, to move your family into the village, to build a house worthy of your standing in the town."

Joshua had heard this argument before, and was ready. "Ah, Robert, you flatter us," he said. "But as my wife knows well, I am as fond of farming as I am of the law. And our house on the Post Road is but a short walk to the town. Still," Joshua turned to face his new friend. "Still, I would be interested in purchasing a small parcel of land behind your house, if you are willing, to construct a building to run my practice from."

But Means had become distracted. He waved to a man pulling up in a wagon filled with other men and barrels, pulled by a team of healthy-looking oxen, with a dozen riders close behind.

"Mr. Maxwell, Thompson!" he cried, but he failed to get the driver's attention, which was focused on steering his team toward the workers assembled in the square. Means shrugged and turned back to Joshua and Abigail.

"That man there, he's my primary source of supply from Boston." Robert gestured toward the wagon, which had come to a halt across the common, allowing the men to jump out. "Thompson Maxwell and his friend John Hancock, they provide most of my goods."

The three watched in silence as Maxwell, fifty yards in front of them, leapt lightly to the ground. He was large, broad-shouldered, and dark-haired, in his early thirties, with a sureness that marked him as the leader of the group. He was joking now, and laughing, milling about easily with the men who had shared the wagon. He had a clear precise voice that could be singled out from the others, even those of a louder volume. If Joshua had been closer, he would have seen Maxwell's eyes: light blue that seemed to radiate sincerity. Eyes that would seem more natural on a woman. It was these three physical traits—a strong physical body, clear commanding voice, and the eyes—that gave him his presence and secured the trust of his fellow militia members.

"Those fellows there," Means said, "they're all militia, every one of them. All members of Captain Crosby's company. And Maxwell, he's their lieutenant. A remarkable man, a soldier since his sixteenth year. But reliable—the only times I can't count on deliveries are on militia days. And even then I don't complain. How could I, when the man is willing to take up arms for the protection of our town?"

Joshua didn't answer. He wondered, still looking across at Maxwell, *What would it take to make me want to bear arms?* Nothing he could imagine. No cause he could yet foresee, except to protect Abigail and their children.

Abigail excused herself as a group of village women passed by, calling out to her to help them with the morning's food. Across the common, the building materials—the wall portions, as well as giant piles of cut and joined posts, beams, and rafters, some as large as eighteen inches square and forty feet long—were scattered here and there. Deacon Barker was bellowing louder now, calling instructions to a group that had grown to more than a hundred men. Thompson Maxwell approached; instantly, he had the deacon's attention: "I see you've brought your militiamen. But what about the rum?" called out the deacon.

There were shouts from the crowd of volunteers. The selectmen had voted to provide eight barrels of the best New England rum for the workers and townspeople.

"You needn't worry, Deacon Barker," Maxwell shouted back. "The barrels are in the wagon along with an extra, donated by Mr. Robert Means and the soldiers of the Amherst militia."

A cheer went up from the workers, who then began falling into teams.

By dusk, a mammoth skeleton towered over the common, its wood glowing in the lengthening shadows. It was securely pegged, seventy-five feet in length and fifty feet tall. With the steeple added, it would rise yet another fifty feet. And it had been done in a day, without incident or injury: no fallen workers, no one hurt or crippled by collapsing beams. It was truly, thought Joshua, still lingering in the crowd, though Abigail had gone home, a spectacular achievement. "The pride of Amherst," he said aloud to himself.

The men turned to the task of finishing what was left of the food and rum. The mood was festive. Footraces and wrestling matches took place between those still with energy to spare. Young Sam Wilkins, the son of the Reverend Mr. Wilkins, took a bet that he could not run around the building with the three-hundred-pound Deacon Barker on his shoulders. He managed it—barely—with the crowd whooping and cheering, then collapsed in a heap.

Finally, with darkness threatening, Mr. Wilkins was lifted onto a platform to offer a prayer of thanks for the blessings of the day. As he finished, the crowd began to splinter into groups, an ocean flowing into smaller and smaller tributaries, as neighbors, friends, and families made their way home through the lowering dusk. Cheerful voices called farewells; children rode on fathers' shoulders. And every head, at least once, turned to look back at the structure that rose, like a giant sentinel, in the dark.

It was well that they looked, and remembered. For what they could not know was sad indeed: that the raising of the meetinghouse would be the last peaceful, public event in Amherst for more than half a decade. And that before those five years were through, the storm clouds of revolution, already roiling in from Boston, would turn neighbor against neighbor with a bitterness that today could not have been imagined.

3

SPRING 1774
AMHERST, NEW HAMPSHIRE

THE CORNER OF JONES ROAD and Mack Hill teemed with people. Horses, wagons, dogs, and food vendors jostled each other for space. It was unseasonably warm for early April. The smells of sweat, baked bread, and animal waste hung heavy in the air. On the steps of the courthouse, the Hillsborough County Clerk, a squat man in black coat and wig, swung a heavy bell in circles over his head. From here and there in the crowd came the voices of children as they sang in time with its clangs:

> "Lawyer, lawyer, come to court,
> Take a piece of bread and pork;
> If the pork is not done
> Take a piece of bread and run."

A jail wagon turned the corner heavily, jolted, and stopped in front of the courthouse. The children fell silent, staring, as eight shackled prisoners were led from the wagon by guards. A young boy, nine or ten, approached the wagon driver, hands open, eyebrows raised. The driver nodded once and put a coin in his hand. The boy took the reins of the first of two horses, untethered it from the wagon, and led the animal slowly away.

Joshua Atherton, registrar of probate for Hillsborough County, stood in the doorway of Jones Tavern, watching cross-armed as the crowd waited for the courthouse to open. Though he had practiced law in New Hampshire for a number of years now, opening day of the county court term never failed to thrill him. There was a sense of collegiality. The anticipation of renewing old bonds and forming new ones as well as a simple, nervous excitement; the vagaries of opening day, no matter how scripted, could never be guessed in advance.

Most of the attorneys, as well as many other litigants in the coming court session, had arrived the day before. Nothing could be more awkward to explain to a client than that his case was defaulted because an attorney was late for "opening call." This was particularly true when the magistrate in charge was as infamous as the one scheduled this week: Judge Wyseman Claggett, known throughout the province as the worst sort of judicial bully, a man who liked nothing better than to torment an attorney whose manners or arguments did not suit him or who failed to show the proper respect.

As a result of this, all the inns in Amherst, as well as many private homes whose owners were in need of extra income, had been filled to overflowing with overnight guests. Captain Hildreth, proprietor of Jones Tavern just across the street from the courthouse, had been the first, as always, to fill up. All his rooms, weeks before, had been spoken for, often with three beds to a room and two or three men to a bed. Joshua smiled quietly at the thought he had now: of attorneys Harvell and Lawrence, perhaps the two biggest men he knew at close to three hundred pounds each, wrestling the blankets from each other in one of Captain Hildreth's beds. His next thought was more of the same: of half a dozen teenage chambermaids, whomever the captain had managed to press into service that week, heating pots of water in the kitchen fireplace for use in the lawyers' baths.

Joshua was deeply thankful: that he lived in town, that he had a wife who cooked and cleaned and loved him, that he did not have

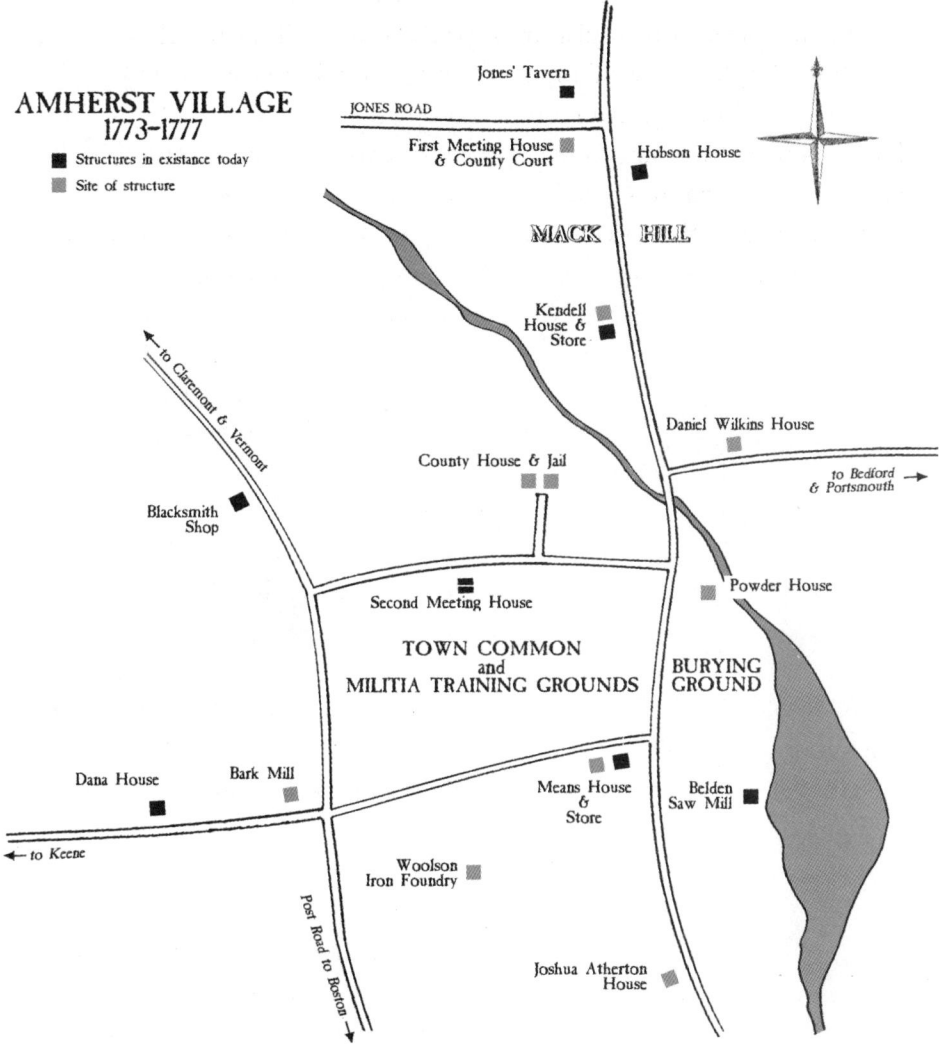

AMHERST VILLAGE
1773–1777

■ Structures in existance today
▨ Site of structure

Jones' Tavern

JONES ROAD

First Meeting House & County Court

Hobson House

MACK HILL

Kendell House & Store

Daniel Wilkins House

to Claremont & Vermont

County House & Jail

to Bedford & Portsmouth

Blacksmith Shop

Second Meeting House

Powder House

TOWN COMMON
and
MILITIA TRAINING GROUNDS

BURYING
GROUND

Dana House

Bark Mill

Means House & Store

Belden Saw Mill

to Keene

Woolson Iron Foundry

Post Road to Boston

Joshua Atherton House

With the relocation of the meetinghouse from the corner of Mack Hill and Jones Road, the area surrounding the town common became the new town center.

15

Jones Tavern
Noted as the second most populated building in Amherst, second only
to the meetinghouse, Jones Tavern was built between 1730 and 1740
and was the first tavern in the village.

to fight a crowd of sleepy, half-drunk attorneys for a simple meal and a bath.

"Joshua, Joshua! Wait for me!" came a call from the stable area.

Turning, he saw none other than Timothy Harvell, arms loaded with books and bundles of pleadings, scurrying furiously, red-faced, to overtake him.

"What a night, what a night we had!" Timothy exclaimed as he drew even with Joshua, puffing so hard the words came out as gasps. "It's too bad you left early, Joshua. You missed the best of the fun."

Joshua's thoughts turned to the night before. There had been a gathering in the tavern—lawyers, judges, clerks—that was beginning to turn rowdy about the time he'd left.

"Well, it was important I return home at a decent hour. Young Charles is ill, and his mother is quite worn out caring for him. But you cannot tell me that our learned brethren became even more inebriated than they were when I left."

"Well, not noticeably," said Timothy after some reflection, falling into step with his colleague, his breathing gradually slowing, his color returning to normal. Joshua slowed his pace to accommodate the larger man, who was obviously eager to tell his version of things.

"But Joshua, just after you left, Judge Claggett—that would be His Excellency, the Right Honorable Wyseman Claggett, formerly Solicitor General for King George"—Timothy's voice fairly dripped with distaste—"arrived from his dinner at the Means mansion. I suppose he would say he came to celebrate the opening of the court session with us, but you know that's rubbish. You should have seen the look on his face when he came through that tavern door"—and here Timothy attempted an impression of Claggett, a lip-quivering, nose-twisting series of poses that made his sweaty face even more comical than before. "You know what a pompous ass he is—and a mean bastard, too."

Joshua laughed and shook his head. Timothy was a lover of gossip, and nearly all of it was harmless. Still, Joshua sometimes won-

dered if he possessed too little discretion for his own good, if he took
enough care when he told his endless stories about those who, if they
chose to, could make his life very difficult indeed. He stopped walking and turned to face his friend. "Timothy—"

But it was no use. There was precious little time before the
courthouse opening, and Timothy was bursting with his tale: "The
judge, when he came in the tavern, he was sporting this new wig.
Very grand, very distinctive. And he was so proud of it, stroking the
bloody thing as though he had a kitten on his head."

Joshua took the bait. "A new wig? Court starts in ten minutes
and you're going to tell me about Claggett's new wig?"

"Hold on. Last night, what do you remember about Gordon?"

"I remember that he was drunk."

"Yes. Drunk. And he got drunker. Much drunker. He got so
drunk he was singing *Yankee Doodle* standing on a chair."

Joshua winced at what he guessed was coming. Gordon had a
nasty side, especially after drink. And he was a Loyalist. Put him in a
room with a man like Claggett, with a few too many ales under his
belt, and things could turn very ugly very fast.

"Well," Timothy went on, "there he was, standing on a chair,
singing *Yankee Doodle* at the top of his lungs to the assembled audi-
ence. Stupid of him, I know—there probably wasn't a Tory in the
place. And Hildreth—isn't he a captain in the Amherst militia or
something?"

Joshua nodded, frowning.

Timothy sighed and continued. "Well, there's Gordon singing
with his back to the door, when who arrives but His Honor, sporting
his new wig. He walks straight to the table Gordon's standing on and
stands there behind him, hands on his hips, as patient as a saint, waiting for the moment when the poor fellow turns around..."

Joshua stood stock-still, waiting. He felt his fists ball. *The fool*, he
thought. *The asinine, unmitigated fool.*

"Well, of course, by now everyone's seen Claggett, and we're all standing there with our mouths open, just waiting for the moment of truth. And finally Gordon, he swings around to see what we're all staring at, and he's singing and his arms are flying around, and he knocks the judge's wig right off his head and into the fireplace! I tell you, it just missed landing in a pot of lamb stew!"

"Then what happened? What did Claggett do?" Joshua was beside himself, staring at the ground at his feet, ready to hear the worst.

"You should have seen his face. I swear, Joshua, it was redder than the coals in the fire. And for a second he was stunned, speechless. His lips were moving but there was nothing coming out. It was something to see. And then he found his voice. 'Gordon, you clumsy bastard!' And he just keeps yelling that, until—"

Timothy stopped briefly, catching his breath, nearly spent from the effort of his tale.

"Until what?" Joshua prodded.

"Well, you know Attorney Charles Smith, that toady?"

Joshua nodded.

"He jumped up and snatched the wig from the coals just as the fringes were beginning to scorch. 'Your wig, Judge, I saved your wig from the fire.' Ugh! It was revolting. Well, Claggett grabbed it without a word, glared at all of us as though we were evil incarnate, and stomped out of the tavern. No one has seen him since."

Joshua stared. Timothy's three hundred pounds were shaking with the effort not to laugh, for he had a sense of Joshua's mood.

"Even worse, Gordon thought it was the joke of the evening. He almost fell off the chair, he was laughing so hard. I think I know what you're thinking—we'll see the results of all this in Claggett's courtroom today."

"We certainly shall," said Joshua. "We certainly shall."

Silently, in the instant that followed, he conjured the results. Gordon would of course be roasted and carved by the judge. His clients were as good as guilty before the court convened—but it was unlikely to end there. Judge Claggett, knowing that word of his toasted wig must surely have spread, would turn his wrath on anyone who so much as looked awry. As solicitor general for the king, he had been among the most aggressive, the most bullying of prosecutors. The fact that he was a recent convert to the cause of liberty would only make Gordon's prank of last night that much more galling.

They continued walking. Joshua gave vent to his thoughts: "Timothy, how would you like to be Gordon in court today?"

Timothy didn't answer, only shook his head and kept walking.

"It always amazes me," said Joshua—he was talking more to himself than to his companion—"how members of such a learned profession can behave like children even when they understand, as surely they must, that there is so very much at stake."

Timothy, looking sheepish, nodded briefly and kept walking.

"Do you remember last fall," said Joshua, "at the call-of-the-list, when someone dropped a garter snake down Gordon's breeches?"

Timothy nodded, then involuntarily began to laugh. Instinctively he checked himself. The two men crossed Jones Road; the courthouse was in sight.

Joshua, no longer attempting an exchange, grew pensive. He recalled a story he had heard about Claggett, told to him by a Portsmouth attorney:

The judge had wanted to purchase firewood for his home. On hearing the price, he had sworn at the woodsman, who, in turn, quite accustomed to such language, responded in kind and stomped out of the judge's home. Within the space of a day, the man had been arrested and brought before Judge Claggett for trial. The charge: public profanity. Knowing that such a case was unwinnable, the woodsman apologized to the judge.

"Squire Claggett harbors malice against no man," said the judge, "and forgives you."

"Thank you, sir," the defendant responded. He turned to leave the court.

"Stop, sir!" the judge then bellowed. "*Squire* Claggett forgives you. But *Judge* Claggett does not!"

Upon the woodcutter, stunned and silent, were then imposed costs and fines to the limits of what the law allowed.

No, thought Joshua. This was not a day to stand in court against Judge Claggett, who even on his best day was impatient and without compassion.

Crossing Jones Road with Timothy beside him, Joshua spied his old friend Benjamin Whiting, sheriff of Hillsborough County, with a deputy unloading prisoners from the wagon in front of the court-house. The men were shackled, arm and leg, an extreme measure, thought Joshua, considering the distance from the jail to court.

The sheriff waved and called him over. "We have your client inside, Joshua." He gestured at the shackles with a helpless look and shrugged: "I don't like to see the doctor in prison any more than you do. He's a good man; he should be home with his family, not in irons."

Joshua nodded. "I realize, Benjamin, that you are only doing what was ordered. Please treat him as well as you can. And tell him, will you, that I'll call at the jail after court."

Joshua and Timothy walked into the courthouse. It was a small structure, only forty-five feet from end to end, that had been built nearly four decades before, when Amherst's population was a tenth of the fourteen hundred it was now. Today it was bulging with bodies. The heat was nearly overpowering. Even the gallery under the rafters was packed as lawyers, witnesses, defendants, and the simply curious elbowed each other for space.

It would be a long day, Joshua knew. First would come the call of the court docket, then the criminal sentencing. Finally pleas, such as his client's, would be heard. There was nothing to do but wait, for he dared not risk being absent and having it be noticed by the judge. It would not be the first time an absent lawyer had resulted in the dismissal of a plea. It was not wise to annoy Claggett. Joshua sat.

Most of the onlookers, he guessed, were here for the sentencing of Jonas Stapleton. Next to murder, a sentencing for theft usually drew the largest crowds.

Moses Eaton, the just-appointed clerk pro tempore, stood and loudly cleared his throat. The din ceased abruptly.

"His Majesty's Court of General Session of the Peace, held in Amherst, in the County of Hillsborough and Province of New Hampshire, is now in session, the Honorable Judge Wyseman Claggett presiding. God save the King!

"The first matter before the Honorable Court is that of the King versus Jonas Stapleton."

Clerk Eaton turned to the prisoner and read the charge. A diminutive, frail-looking man, Stapleton had been helped to his feet by the sheriff's deputy. He looked for all the world as though he could barely support the weight of the chains on his arms and legs. He turned his head upward to hear his fate.

Judge Claggett, a large man with heavy black hair, glared down at him through his narrow dark eyes. "You are charged with stealing goods owned by Nahum Baldwin. How say you? Are you guilty?"

Without giving the prisoner a second to respond, Claggett suddenly leaned forward, both hands flat on the bench top, and bellowed: "You know you are. You were seen in the act. The goods were found in your house. Be a man. Admit your crime and spare this court the wasted time."

Joshua heard the sudden intake of breath next to him and a low whisper, "That cruel bastard," and he remembered that Timothy was sitting next to him. He glanced quickly at Timothy, then at Stapleton. He was sure the man would swoon. He was shaking and moaning. It was clear he was in poor health, probably also, Joshua suspected, of limited intelligence. All he managed was a single, barely audible "Yes."

"What? I cannot hear you—speak up!" Claggett rose from his chair to a half-standing position and leaned forward toward the prisoner, whose response this time was only a trace louder than before: "Yes, sir. Guilty, sir."

Now it was the clerk's turn: "Address the judge as 'Your Honor,' and please speak in a voice the court can hear." Young Eaton, it seemed, was enjoying his small part in the proceedings.

But Claggett waved him aside impatiently. "I accept your plea of guilty. You understand," he paused—"the sentences for theft that this court can render are several." He paused once more, this time longer. When he resumed, his voice was deeper and more deliberate, almost disembodied, devoid of any humanness at all: "One, flogging on your naked back, ten to fifty lashes. Two, a lengthy time in jail. Three, the branding of the letter 'T' on your forehead. Four, restitution of the stolen goods. Or all four." Claggett's eyes gleamed. "What say you?"

Joshua thought Stapleton would surely faint—a second prisoner was now supporting him. There was a brief commotion in the vicinity of the court's entrance; all eyes turned to see the Reverend Mr. Daniel Wilkins enter the room.

Not a man to be easily cowed, Mr. Wilkins moved forward to the table that served as the bench and addressed the court without pausing for breath: "Your Honor, I ask that I may speak for Mr. Stapleton."

Judge Claggett, scowling but apparently not willing to publicly insult Amherst's most venerable minister, nodded. "You understand that under the king's law the prisoner has no right to have one speak for him But I consent in this instance," he said.

Mr. Wilkins nodded perfunctorily, then began: "I have known Mr. Stapleton for a number of years. He has committed a wrong, and acknowledges his fault. However, to brand him or sentence him to prison will only harm his wife and children, who are in need of his income, small as it is."

The minister paused, allowing his words to hang in the courtroom. Joshua guessed that he was counting on one of Claggett's well-publicized views: that government should offer little or no assistance to the needy, as it would increase the tax burden on citizens such as himself.

"Imprisoning Mr. Stapleton would keep him from work," Mr.Wilkins went on. "Branding would be even worse; he would be prevented from obtaining employment in the future. Either punishment would result in his family becoming a ward of the county, a burden to those who pay its taxes."

Joshua leaned forward, curious to see the effect on the judge of the minister's careful words.

"Thank you, Mr. Wilkins." Claggett, for the next several seconds, could be seen to be scribbling; he then handed the paper to his clerk. Mr. Wilkins cast Stapleton a reassuring glance. The clerk stood, walked forward a step or two, and cleared his throat: "Jonas Stapleton, you are accused of stealing and have pled guilty. It is the sentence of this court that you be whipped twenty stripes on the naked back at the public whipping post on Amherst Common, between the hours of one and two this next day. Further, you are ordered to pay Nahum Baldwin, the owner of the goods stolen, the sum of forty-four pounds lawful money, being ten times the value of the goods taken and costs of prosecution. If you fail to pay the damages, the said Nahum Baldwin is authorized to dispose of you in the servitude of any of His Majesty's subjects for a period of up to seven years, to commence from this day."

The Reverend Mr. Wilkins leapt to his feet. "Your Honor, the goods taken have been returned whole and undamaged!"

"Mr. Wilkins, I will hear no more from you. The sentence was fair. It will not be changed. Sheriff, remove the prisoner."

As if both Stapleton and Mr. Wilkins had ceased to exist, Claggett now turned his attention to Joshua. "Attorney Atherton, I have read your petition and see no merit in it, but I will give you a brief moment of the court's time. Remember, we have many other matters for today."

Joshua, his attention still lingering on the spectacle of the min-

utes just passed, remained seated for a moment, gripping the sides of
the bench beneath him, mustering his wits. Then he sighed deeply,
just once, and rose slowly to his feet. The judge, he knew, was in a
rage. It would not end with Stapleton. No client, no defendant,
would be spared his wrath this day.

Perhaps, thought Joshua, if Claggett had not recently renounced
his Loyalist feelings to join the Whig cause—he had announced his
conversion barely a month ago—perhaps then, as a fellow Loyalist, he
might benefit from a measure of partisan sympathy. But no longer.
Now, even politics was a wedge between them.

Then he thought of the charred wig. For a man such as Claggett,
there could be no provocation to match the wounding of pride.
Silently, as he rose in his place to speak, Joshua damned his friend
Gordon for what last night's drunkenness, before this day was over,
was likely to cost them all.

"Did you speak, Attorney Atherton? If so, please, a little louder,
so that I may hear you!" thundered the voice from the bench.

"No, Your Honor, I was just collecting myself." Joshua fumbled
with his robe, smiled thinly, and shuffled his feet.

"Well, get on with it then. And speak up."

"Yes, Your Honor. May it please the court, I am Joshua Atherton,
and here to represent Doctor Mussey . . ."

"Yes, I know that. On with it!" The judge leaned forward,
smacked the desk in front of him with the flat of his hand, and
scowled at Joshua, dark eyes peering menacingly from beneath the
heavy hair and brows.

"Your Honor, I appreciate that the court has read my petition,
but I ask that I may describe my client and his acts. It is possible that
I did not include all the facts in the petition, or that the petition may
have smudges so that portions may not be clearly readable."

This, of course, was pure fabrication. Joshua was nothing if not
meticulous in the preparation of his petitions. However, it was widely held that Judge Claggett left unread at least some of the writs put

before him. It would certainly explain his hasty judgments. Justice was always easier if the facts were not there to cloud the case.

"My client, Dr. John Mussey, is an honorable and eminent member of the Amherst community. As a doctor, his services are greatly needed. There are far too few physicians in Hillsborough County to have one languishing in jail for a small sum and a matter of principle."

"If he is in prison for debt, then why does he not pay the debt?" the judge retorted. "A small sum, you say. Then why not pay it, return to his medical practice, and all in the community would benefit? Why is this matter taking up time in this court session, Attorney Atherton, if your client is as honorable as you say and his debt so very small? Why? Attorney Atherton? Kindly answer me that." The judge's voice was rising ominously. Joshua knew that his remaining time was short.

"True, Your Honor. Very true. It is a small sum, yet also a matter of principle. It is well known, is it not, that this court has the reputation for fairness and understanding in matters of honor and principle?" He hoped his appeal to Claggett's ego was not as transparent as it felt.

"Go on, Attorney Atherton. But be brief."

"Thank you, Your Honor. Doctor Mussey is a Presbyterian; he pays for the expenses of his church through his donations every Sunday. Therefore, he objected to the cost of the Congregational church and its ministers being added to his town tax bill every year. The first year, the parish portion of his tax bill was seventy-five cents; the next year, one pound. Doctor Mussey was ordered to pay these sums, but refused, as a matter of principle. He has been arrested and placed in the Amherst jail, even shackled to the prison wall at night. You see him in court today, Your Honor, in irons, like a common vagrant or thief."

"Attorney Atherton, I am a member of His Majesty's Church of England and pay for its upkeep from my earnings, but still I pay my taxes knowing that a portion is being directed to the Congregational church. I accept this as my duty. Why does your client not pay this paltry amount and be done with the matter?" The judge's voice was rising once again.

"Because, Your Honor, it is not the sum but the issue of religious freedom that is important to my client. Even in England, King George is said to be recognizing the freedom to worship; it is said to be a wave sweeping across Europe and England. I pray that the court will be sympathetic, that it acknowledge the principle involved in this matter, and that it free Doctor Mussey from jail. Allow him to pursue his dispute through the court as a free man, rather than as a prisoner. You have seen for yourself the dismal conditions of the Amherst jail. This is all I have to say. I rest, and leave this matter to the wisdom of the court."

As he seated himself, Joshua felt that he had at least won the judge's attention. Interruptions from the bench had been fewer and briefer toward the end. Possibly, he thought, Claggett's rage was spent. He was quiet for the moment, looking thoughtful, no doubt considering the merits of the issue at hand. Joshua held his breath and waited.

"Attorney Atherton, you have spoken eloquently on behalf of your client." Joshua nodded his thanks

"But I am not convinced." Claggett's brow descended again. "You have quoted no law. I might be otherwise inclined if the amount were not so trivial. I am of the feeling that Doctor Mussey is flouting the law. Many citizens, including myself, are not Congregationalist. All of us, as far as I know, pay our full taxes, the church portion not excepted.

"Doctor Mussey will remain in jail until he reimburses the town for his delinquent taxes and this court its costs."

"But Your Honor," Joshua rose and took a step forward.

"No. No. There is nothing further to be said. Your petition is denied. Take your seat, Attorney Atherton, so that we may hear the next matter before we adjourn for lunch."

As he reached the door a few moments later, a tap on his shoulder caused Joshua to turn around. "A moment of your time, please, Joshua," the voice behind him said. He turned to face Mr. Wilkins. "Joshua, if you are traveling back to the common, I'll walk with you as far as my house."

Daniel Wilkins was one of the earliest settlers in town. He had come as its first Congregational minister—ordained in this very same meetinghouse—in 1741, when it had held only fourteen families and was called Souhegan West. He was part of its past. Its people, and its future, were important to his heart.

As he and Joshua Atherton walked their horses down Mack Hill toward the site of the new village center, Mr. Wilkins considered carefully what words he would speak. He could see that the attorney was still choking on his defeat; he elected to keep silent for another few minutes, to give him more time to put aside his anger. This was typical of Mr.Wilkins; he was a prudent, patient man.

They walked by Kendall's store, greeting Nathan Kendall, who was overseeing the unloading of supplies from a wagon parked in front. Kendall, whose store traffic more than doubled during the opening of court every spring, waved cheerfully as they passed. On the other side, the minister caught sight of Thompson Maxwell, and realized that the wagon must be his.

"Good day, Mr. Maxwell," he said, noting without surprise the curt nod that passed between Maxwell and Joshua Atherton. It saddened him, this Whig Loyalist bitterness that, he feared, would rend Amherst fully in two before it was likely to end. There were times when he wanted nothing so much as to take men like Atherton and Maxwell by their ears, as he would a pair of scuffling boys, and insist that they make peace. Was he the only one who could see that in men such as these two, at least, the love of freedom and the right to choose ran equally strong? That both were worthy values? And that political divisions were as nothing next to these?

The two men continued walking. They were a minute or so past Kendall's store before the minister finally spoke: "Joshua, I do thank you for your efforts to assist Doctor Mussey."

Joshua nodded, but remained silent. He knew there was more to come.

"While I would not have agreed with him a few years ago," Mr. Wilkins continued, "I think now that he has a valid point. New Hampshire is a small colony, and mostly poor. Our citizens cannot afford to support the Congregational church with their tax dollars. Nor should they be made to—especially those who are already giving, voluntarily, to support other denominations. It's simply not right. There is no exclusivity in God. The church has no place in town government."

"The movement of religious freedom is gaining strength in England, Mr.Wilkins," replied Joshua, "as well as here. But surely"— and here he paused briefly, put his hand on the other man's elbow, and smiled—"surely, complimenting me on a position of law is not the only reason you sought my company?"

The minister slowed his walk, almost stopping. The two men's eyes met and held.

"No, Joshua, it isn't. The tension I noticed a few moments ago between you and Thompson Maxwell gives me even further reason to want to air my thoughts. You have been a resident of Amherst, and a member of our congregation, for only a little more than a year, but you have gained the respect of most of the town, despite your Loyalist views. I feel, though, that I must caution you—you are doing yourself and your family no service by publicly espousing them. You cannot help but know of the tensions that are building throughout the colonies, and Amherst is no exception.

"You seem to make a point of letting everyone know your opinions. Not all of them take well to this; there are rumors, Joshua, of threats overheard in nearby towns to burn your property, to tar and feather you, to subject you to a public inquisition regarding your loyalty to King George."

Joshua sighed. He had heard all this before, though never, perhaps, with quite such force.

"What would you have me do, Mr. Wilkins? Play the hypocrite? Lie? Ignore a matter that could destroy our way of life and the land I love?"

"No, Joshua, I would not have you be false to your own beliefs. But I do know that although many of our other citizens, including a number of those of your own profession, share your views, they do not find it necessary, however, as you seem to, to express them publicly. They confine themselves to speaking among family and friends, and in private. Which, I don't think I have to tell you, I believe is the wisest course.

"You are aware, Joshua, that the winds of change are gathering in our colonies. They may be a breeze or a hurricane, no one can yet know which. But one thing is certain. The king cannot continue forever on this course of dictating, not giving us any say in our lives. People want the same rights as Englishmen: to vote, to have a voice in what happens to them. What took place in Boston, with the tea— it cannot be erased, it will have repercussions.

"But in the meantime, Joshua, there is no need to be so defiant, no need to speak out publicly against the beliefs of most of your neighbors. It can only bring grief to your family."

He hesitated. Then he joined his fingers together, as though, perhaps, in prayer. But it wasn't prayer. His index fingers formed an arrow, which, as he spoke, tapped rhythmically against his chin. He was thinking carefully, considering his words: "I have even heard talk that General Gage intends to raid all of the powder houses in the New England colonies and remove our supply of powder and shot."

Joshua exploded. "That's hogwash, hogwash! Just the sort of lies and half-truths that come from Thompson Maxwell when he returns from one of his Boston trips! Those Boston hotheads—Adams and Hancock—they manipulate him like the puppet that he is!"

The minister wasn't cowed by the outburst.

"Perhaps you should give him, and his opinions, more credit, Joshua. Thompson Maxwell is not an unintelligent man. He may be a teamster, and less well educated than you, but he holds his beliefs as strongly as you do yours. Like many people, he feels that freedom and self-determination are the rights of the colonies. He has been a soldier for a long time, Joshua, and seen much suffering and danger. He would not enter into conflict lightly, and would not fight over something he did not hold dear."

Joshua studied the minister's face. "I take it he has reached your ear as well."

Daniel Wilkins did not answer immediately. Then he laid a hand on Joshua's shoulder, where he left it for the duration of his speech: "Joshua, I ask you to carefully consider what I am about to say—for your sake, as well as for Abigail and your children.

"Fifteen years ago, during the French and Indian War, towns throughout New Hampshire were subjected to Indian attacks. We blamed the French for instituting the savagery, and I saw what mobs can do—what they did to some French families in the area. All good people, loving families, but with the misfortune of tracing their ancestry to France.

"Now, once again, I see conflict arising and sides being taken, Loyalist against patriot. I fear it will result in similar retribution, similar violence, and the loss of life not only on the battlefield but also in our very own villages, between friends and families, among ourselves. I urge you, Joshua, to put aside your hatred. Do not be part of such a thing."

Joshua listened carefully. His anger softened. And it was with a thoughtful tone that he addressed the minister.

"I agree with much of what you say, Mr.Wilkins," he said. "Much harm has been done on both sides. The massacre in Boston was surely a tragedy, but Maxwell and his friends did not help matters with that 'tea party,' as they called it, last year.

"I see our colonies as having limitless possibilities. England is old and we are young, but we cannot win a conflict with the greatest army and navy in the world. And what will happen if we remain on the course we are on? It seems only logical—the king will impose military rule on all of us, not only the port of Boston. There will be an English army outpost in every city and town."

Joshua shook his head. "No, Mr. Wilkins. The patriots, as you say, may be well intentioned, and I do not doubt that their principles are as strong as you claim, but they are wrong, wrong. Instead of these childish, pointless displays of defiance, we must show our willingness to compromise with the crown.

"We could begin by paying the cost of that tea. In this way, and others, I believe we could demonstrate—if it is not already too late—that we remain the king's subjects. For it will only be as subjects that we can gain the rights we seek.

"If we continue as we are, if we pursue matters as Thompson Maxwell and the others would have us do, we will be subjecting ourselves and our families to a conflict we cannot hope to win."

The two men were approaching the bottom of Mack Hill, close to the intersection of Bedford Road, only minutes from the minister's home. The men stood for a moment. The minister's voice, for the first time since they had begun their walk, betrayed the urgency he felt.

"No, Joshua," he said. "No. I pray you, listen to the wisdom of an old man. The die is cast—there will be conflict. You have only to look to Portsmouth, to what has happened there. Last December, the governor refused to allow the New Hampshire Assembly to form a Committee of Correspondence, which would have given us closer ties with the other colonies. The assembly ignored him and formed one anyway. The only choice the governor had was to dissolve the assembly. But almost to a man, as the members walked down the street after being ejected from the province house, they decided the assembly had not been dissolved but only adjourned, so they reconvened in a nearby tavern. When Wentworth heard of this ultra vires assembly, he had his sheriff eject the men from the tavern. Still, they were not deterred. They moved down the road to Exeter and formed the new people's government. Wentworth knows he has lost control, that he has no effective government. And the people of New Hampshire know it, too. They know they are too independent, and too many, to control. It can end only one way."

Joshua shook his head in exasperation. "Mr.Wilkins! This proves my point, that we need to work toward showing the king that we are his subjects or the next thing we know British troops will be in Portsmouth as well. Don't the people see that they are only decreasing their freedoms this way?"

The minister sounded resigned. "I do not agree with you, Joshua, though I respect your views. However, my most serious concern at the moment is you."

He paused, staring at a point somewhere over Joshua's shoulder. When he spoke again, his voice was newly soft: "Experience tells me that no matter who wins this struggle, life will be harder for you, as a known Loyalist, than it ever was before. The majority of the population will resent you, win or lose, for no other reason than that the Loyalists are those who hold influence and have prospered under the king's rule—the wealthy merchants who deal in trade with England, the political appointees such as you. It will be the resentment of those who have little of those who have much. Not to mention, as in your case, the feelings the public bears toward attorneys these days."

Joshua seemed weary of talking. "Mr. Wilkins, I hope that reason will prevail and that you will be proved wrong."

The two were silent as they reached the bottom of Mack Hill. The minister's home was to their left. Joshua would leave him to continue up to the new meetinghouse, and from there to his office. As they parted, Mr. Wilkins made his final plea: "I know I cannot change your views," he said. "But please, for the sake of your family, be careful. Practice moderation. Be selective in whom you speak with. Be prudent in what you say."

Joshua smiled and extended his hand. The minister took it.

"I know you mean well, Mr. Wilkins. And you may be right. Still, I cannot help but speak my conscience. I will not be a hypocrite."

"God keep you well, then," said the minister, as he turned to leave. "God keep you safe."

4

DECEMBER 16, 1773
BOSTON

THE TRIP SEEMED to be taking longer than usual. Even so, he was still ahead of schedule. It was not the time, he reasoned, but rather his own discomfort, that was causing anxiety.

The light morning rain had soaked through his jacket; the wetness, coupled with the winter cold, had made the day seem very long. He glanced over his shoulder, thinking he could detect some clearing in the northwestern sky, and tried to take comfort from that.

He could make the trip in his sleep. Even the oxen could probably follow the route without help. He glanced again behind him, this time to make certain that the freight in his wagon was secure, then let his mind drift.

It took him to the evening before: to the warmth and good company of his brother-in-law, Jonathan Wilson, a captain in the militia of Bedford, Massachusetts, whose home—midway between Boston and Amherst—was his guarantee of a bed to break up the trip.

Last night, like many in the past, he and Jonathan, along with four or five fellows from the Bedford militia, had passed the evening at Fitch's Tavern, regaling one another with ten-year-old stories and trading accounts of the latest news, which, in its way, was as precious a

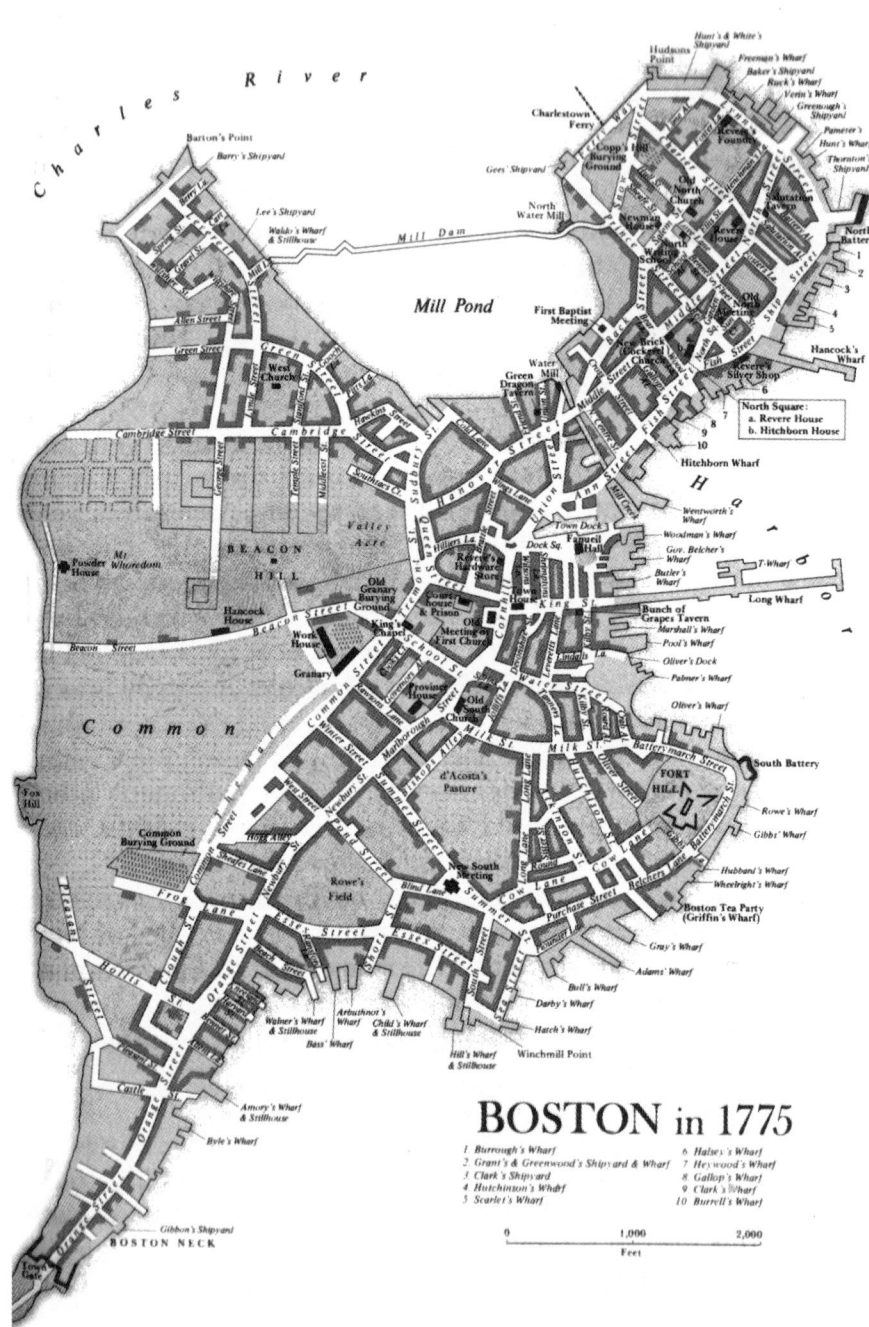

BOSTON in 1775

1. Burrough's Wharf
2. Grant's & Greenwood's Shipyard & Wharf
3. Clark's Shipyard
4. Hutchinson's Whdrf
5. Scarlet's Wharf

6. Halsey's Wharf
7. Heywood's Wharf
8. Gallop's Wharf
9. Clark's Wharf
10. Burrell's Wharf

0   1,000   2,000
            Feet

commodity to carry back to Amherst as any of the freight that he bore. "Damn!"

Thompson Maxwell was jolted from his reveries by the sight of a squad of British soldiers between him and the Cambridge bridge. They were stopping travelers. "Damn!" he muttered again, thinking how close he had come to choosing instead to cross the Charles at Watertown. But who could have known? Who could have guessed that the British had a company here?

He drew nearer to the clot of wagons and carts that blocked his way, trying as he maneuvered to figure out what was going on. From a hundred yards, he could make out the red uniform of a British officer—spotless, the telltale sign of a soldier new to the colonies—who was bellowing indiscriminately, seemingly to everyone at once. He reeked of arrogance, like so many of the king's officers, and viewed the approaching wagon with disdain.

Thompson pulled up, the oxen shuffling, then finally halting, one hundred feet short of the bridge. The officer approached him stiffly.

Several of his soldiers walked immediately to the wagon, lifted the canvas backing, and poked their heads inside.

"What are you transporting? What is your destination?"

"I carry a load of farm produce from Amherst, New Hampshire, to John Hancock's warehouse in Boston." As soon as the words were out of his mouth, Thompson cursed himself.

"Hancock! That bastard!" said the officer. "Get off the wagon! Get off the wagon now!"

The officer spat, then turned to face his men. "Give it a thorough search! Every basket! Every box!"

Four regulars climbed on the back of the wagon and began their search. Thompson tried not to react as he watched basket after basket of vegetables upended and hurled to the ground, many then stepped on and squashed, some by the officer, who seemed to take pleasure in it.

His trip to Boston, thought Thompson, would be a total loss.

There might be one consolation: if this senselessness, this wanton-ness, served to harden Mr. Hancock's already bitter hatred of the king. His anger softened by the thought, Thompson pursed his lips and awaited the order to remount.

On finding nothing illegal, or even of great value, the officer became more agitated, shoving Thompson rudely while giving the order: "Repack and get out of the way!"

Thompson stumbled on the edge of the frozen road. The soldiers snickered. Climbing onto the wagon in far too much haste, he real-ized that he had torn his trousers on a spoke. The soldiers, seeing this, pointed at his half-naked calf and laughed uproariously.

Guiding his pillaged wagon across the Cambridge bridge, Thompson tried to recall if he had ever in his life felt such hate.

John Hancock, arriving at the Old South Meeting Hall just after ten that morning, had been astonished by the size of the crowd outside. Two hundred citizens at least, a sure sign that the hall inside would be bursting. And none of the two hundred, for all the growing force of the frigid winter rain, seemed inclined to be anywhere but here.

Every one of them, Hancock knew without thinking, had come for a single purpose: to await the arrival of Thomas Rotch, captain and owner of the schooner *Dartmouth*, who was to announce his intentions for the shipment of tea stored in his hold.

Hancock didn't like the choices left to Captain Rotch. If he yield-ed to the citizens' demands to set sail out of Boston Harbor with the tea still unloaded, he would be sunk by English cannon at the harbor entrance before he reached the open sea. If he failed to set sail, the king's revenue officers, whose duty it was to collect taxes on the tea, would board his ship forcibly and unload his freight to the con-signees—and Rotch himself, if the citizens' threats could be believed, would be in peril of losing his life and having the *Dartmouth* burned. Small wonder, thought Hancock, that the man has delayed his arrival to our hall.

Once inside, he caught sight of Sam Adams, who stood toward the front, just under the raised podium. He made his way to Adam's side.

"Any sign of the captain yet?"

"None, of course," Adams answered. He smiled a bit grimly. "The captain, I fear, is in a devil of a fix."

"Yes, but the customs deadline, the twenty days, is up tomorrow. If he hasn't unloaded his tea by then—"

"John, John, we must allow matters to take their course. We have come too far to consider turning back. Let's take our places. Samuel Savage is presiding. The captain will be along in time."

The two men took their seats in the front, as Savage climbed to the podium. Almost immediately there arose a chorus of shouts from the rear of the hall: "Send the king his tea!" "No more taxes!" "Damn the clearance!"

"Citizens, citizens!" Savage was doing his best to preside. "Citizens, please! The captain has arrived."

The room fell silent. Captain Rotch, looking exhausted and defeated and a full decade older than his thirty-five years, began haltingly. No, he said, he had not altered his thinking: He could not leave the harbor without official clearance. The British had ordered the sinking of any ship attempting to leave the harbor without permission. It would mean the loss of the *Dartmouth* and his own financial ruin. And no, he was not willing to protest the customhouse decision.

An angry buzz filled the hall. Savage, once again, called for order, this time with less success.

It was a half hour before the matter was resolved: Rotch would go to Milton, to the governor's country estate. Once there, he would demand from Governor Hutchinson a permit for safe passage of the *Dartmouth* out of Boston Harbor. He would return with the governor's decision as quickly as he could.

The captain, less than pleased at the prospect of a seven-mile ride in the cold and rain, was sent on his way. The meeting was adjourned, to reconvene that afternoon at three o'clock. They would await the news from Rotch.

John Hancock, watching the captain make his way through the crowd at the back of the hall, couldn't resist a pang of sympathy. There was little likelihood, he knew, that the governor would yield to the demands of those he was fond of referring to as "the Boston rabble." There would be no safe passage. The citizens, in the end, would decide this matter themselves, as was the plan.

Crossing Dorchester Neck, through the town gate and into the city of Boston at a few minutes past one in the afternoon, Thompson Maxwell was still trying—so far to no avail—to prevent his mood from being fouled by the incident at the bridge. The Neck, a narrow strip of land without which the city itself would have been an island, was a point of congestion for travelers; it sometimes caused Thompson as much as an hour's delay. Today, though, there was no great traffic; he passed through with his wagon in just a few minutes.

He came off the Neck onto the head of Newbury Street, then to Marlborough, finally to Fish. His route now, for the first time all day, was slowed by other travelers: horses and wagons, oxcarts, single riders, men and women on foot. He slowed often to permit others to cross or pass.

At the head of Fish Street, John Hancock's warehouse came into sight. Thompson's spirits lifted. Despite the delay, he had made good progress. The church bells tolled two. There would be company and conversation at the Green Dragon Tavern that night; Christopher Witham would be there, no doubt, and Patrick Smith, and others he had met through Hancock in the past. There was little chance of boredom in that company; almost any man there had a story to tell—of plots, insurrections, the makings of revolution, all the things that stirred Thompson's blood.

He was a military man, after all, for sixteen years, since the first days of the Indian War. And a patriot: The English, to his mind, were the worst sort of imperialists; their presence in the colonies could not end soon enough for him.

And to be in the company of John Hancock, among the spiritual leaders of the revolutionary movement, a one-man fount of anti-Loyalist zeal, thought Thompson, would surely be a privilege. And an education, too. He straightened in his seat and flicked the reins.

There was an unusually large crowd outside the warehouse, two or three times the number that Thompson was accustomed to seeing. His eyes picked out Hancock: tall, thick-set, and bespectacled, in the center of a circle of men just outside the warehouse doors. It was a spirited group—a dozen men all talking at once. There is something in the air, thought Thompson.

A minute later, now in the center of the circle, he recounted his waylaying by the English, the ruin of his produce, all the events of his day. Hancock listened and at first said nothing; Thompson awaited an outburst. What followed instead, remarkably, was a laugh.

"Don't worry yourself, Thompson. We'll locate a good load to send you back with. And anyway," Hancock paused briefly, then swiveled his head to include the other men in his group, "King George won't be troubling us for long." He smiled. "I'll have someone look after your team and wagon. We have an interesting evening in store. Some sport, if you like."

Thompson studied him, uncertain, then gave voice to what was on his mind: "A man could get hanged on Boston Common for having an interesting evening with you, Mr. Hancock."

Hancock seemed delighted by this. He clapped Thompson hard on the shoulder, then, laughing again, turned to address the group: "We have a volunteer from New Hampshire," he said. "And a tea drinker, at that!"

Thompson looked around in confusion. The men laughed, as much at his bewilderment as at anything Hancock had said. Then he noticed something else: At least four of them had paint-smeared faces; there were Indian headdresses in the hands of several men.

Something was afoot. Thompson felt the briefest wave of fear. Then it passed: John Hancock was a man to be admired, both personally and in business; he was bold but also careful. If he was instigating something, he was certain to have thought it through.

Hancock was calling to one of his men to tend to Thompson's wagon and oxen. That done, he steered him toward a third man and introduced the two: "Samuel Meade, this is Thompson Maxwell, a friend and colleague from Amherst, New Hampshire. One of Rogers's Rangers in the Indian War. Take him to the tavern and see if you can find a few feathers for him."

As Meade led him away, laughing like the others at his confusion, Thompson heard Hancock announce to his men: "I must return to the meeting hall. Captain Rotch is due back. We must allow them their full remedies before it is time to act."

But by three o'clock, the appointed hour, the captain had yet to show his face. The crowd, if possible, was thicker than before. And angrier.

"I don't like this," the moderator, Samuel Savage, whispered to Samuel Adams on the podium, where they sat with other members of the Committee of Safety. "We can't expect them to wait forever. They won't be still for long."

"Let's speak to them, then," said Adams, "and ensure at least that our purpose is well known."

One by one, the leaders arose—Adams, Hancock, Savage, Joseph Warren, and Thomas Young—to reiterate their opposition to the tea tax and to implore the crowd to wait. For a while, the hall was orderly; proposals were forwarded, arguments were made and heard. Still no sign of Captain Rotch.

By five o'clock, when Josiah Quincy Jr. rose to launch a tirade against the "enemies of America," peace in the hall was again fragile.

"They are not far from violence," Hancock said to Adams. "This is not the way we planned it. Let's disband the meeting and hope for the best."

At 5:15 a vote was taken. Captain Rotch was given an hour's extension. The meeting was officially adjourned. Not a single man left the hall.

It was a long walk through Dock Square, by Fanueil Hall, to the corner of King and Kirby Streets—from John Hancock's warehouse to the Bunch of Grapes tavern. Thompson, in the company of Samuel Meade and five others from the warehouse, was mostly silent along the way. The rest were in a jovial mood; the time passed quickly.

Two of the men still wore at least part of their Indian costumes; Thompson wondered that such dress seemed to stir little interest from passersby. He noticed how few English soldiers there were on the streets—a half-dozen off-duty strollers, a single three-man patrol—and wondered if the weather had kept the men indoors. It was late afternoon and turning colder. It would be dark in an hour, he thought.

They arrived at the tavern at a few minutes before four. Meade and the others exchanged greetings with the innkeeper, and were ushered to a table in the back. The warmth from the large fireplace was powerful; the smells were of wood smoke, damp clothing, tobacco, and rank bodies. Thompson was relieved to be off the street and out of view of the English patrols; his soldierly instincts ran deep. He took a seat, stretched out his legs straight before him, and did his best to relax. But that would be hard. Even before the pitchers of rum and hard cider had arrived at the table, the six men around him were deep in the throes of debate.

"This will not sit well with the king!" the quietest of the six put in now. He had spoken barely a word all the way to the tavern; Thompson had wondered if he knew the others at all. "The Tea Act has cut the price of tea nearly in half—does that not count for anything at all?"

Meade stared at the man with a mix of patience and faint disdain, then he spoke. "Oh, Thompson, Thompson," he said, "you really don't see, do you? The East India Company has a surplus. They can sell their tea for ninepence a pound if they choose. Yes, the tea will be cheap for you and me, but what of our merchants? And the ship owners who carry their stock? They will be driven out of business. They can't compete at that price!"

"Benjamin Franklin himself has denounced the Tea Act!" said another man.

And so it went. For the better part of an hour, the six men sipped rum and talked tea: the seduction of low prices, the loss of liberties, the subversion of free trade. One man spoke of the three ships docked in Boston Harbor—the *Dartmouth*, the *Eleanor*, and the *Beaver*—and how the Committee of Safety had placed them under guard to ensure that no tea reached the docks. Another offered his account of the recent meeting at Faneuil Hall. More than five thousand citizens had turned out, and the vote was to send the tea back to England in the boats in which it had come. There was angry talk of Governor Hutchinson, who had issued the order to fire on any ships that left port without clearance, and much speculation as to the dilemma of Captain Rotch.

Other than his home in Rhode Island, his entire wealth was in the *Dartmouth*. To unload the tea would probably result in the destruction of the ship by the Boston mob; if he attempted to sail from the harbor without permission, the ship would be sunk by cannon fire. Either decision would ruin him.

Thompson said little. He asked at one point what effect all this would have on the small towns of New Hampshire. The answer he got—from the only lawyer in the group, a man named John Right— was, "If we tolerate tyranny in the port of Boston, it will spread like a fever to every colony, every county, every town!"

The more he listened, the more Thompson's passions were inflamed. These were good men: wise, courageous, honest, with a firm commitment to justice and a strong sense of right and wrong. He could be fond of them, he thought to himself. He could share their dreams for the future, he could adopt their causes as his own.

Whether he could fight with them, if it came to that, was another matter. He would have to know more. He would have to convince himself that Amherst had as much at stake in this matter as Boston, that his own livelihood and liberties were as much in peril as theirs.

Still, he was a soldier. He had fought and been wounded, once already, in the name of sovereignty. It was not difficult to imagine, if the men's beliefs proved right, that he might live to do so again.

"Are you with us tonight, Mr. Maxwell?"

It was Samuel Meade, sitting to his left at the table, his hand resting firmly on Thompson's forearm. The question interrupted his thoughts.

"I'm not certain. What is it you propose?"

As Meade went on to explain the scheme, Thompson felt his ardor kindled: all the old tensions, the old energy, the old passions for a fight.

"I can't be certain," he heard himself say again. But there was no firmness in his words. He guessed that, when the time came, he would heft his share of tea.

A cry rose from the back of the Old South Meetinghouse. At fifteen minutes before six o'clock, a quarter-hour short of the agreed-upon deadline, Capt. Francis Rotch had returned. The sky outside was the color of old ashes. Inside, not a single seat was empty; scarcely a foot of wall space in the rear of the hall was not covered by the figure of a man.

The captain, damp, unkempt, and exhausted, was ushered unceremoniously, by the elbows, through the crowd to the front of the room. Slowly, with effort, he mounted the platform and turned to face the crowd. Samuel Savage fell back to allow his presence at the forefront. Every eye was on him. The hall was quiet as a church.

"The governor has refused my plea." The words were halting, but clearly audible. "He has refused to grant safe passage for the *Dartmouth*."

Boston Tea Party

England considered the event vandalism and a wanton destruction of personal property; to the Sons of Liberty it was a statement against King George's control over America's freedom.

"Seize him! Seize him!" A single voice burst like a musket shot from the back, followed instantly by a dozen more: "Seize him!" "Seize him!" "He is ours!"

Rotch did not move, but cast his eyes about fearfully, then lowered them and stood resignedly, awaiting whatever came next.

Samuel Savage pounded his gavel. By the third report, the hall had gone from raucous to restive; by the fifth, there was the semblance of quiet. Thomas Young arose from the back of the platform, took several steps forward, and stood by the captain's side: "This man has done everything in his power to comply with our demands," he said. "I ask that neither Francis Rotch nor anything in his possession be taken or harmed in any way."

Savage then approached the wretched Rotch. "Captain Rotch, we must ask you again, will you order your ship back to England tonight, with the tea still on board?"

"I cannot. It would ruin me."

"Then, Captain Rotch, do you plan to unload the tea?"

This time there was a pause before his answer. "Only on the insistence of the authorities, and then only to protect myself."

Samuel Adams was the next to speak. He rose to his feet, his face grave, his eyes searching the room. "I do not see what more this meeting can do to save us from further tyranny."

A great cry arose. War whoops rang from the gallery, mingled with a medley of cries: "Griffin's Wharf!" "Savages on the docks!" "The Mohawks are coming tonight!"

A man in the rear could be heard above the din: "Who knows how tea will mix with salt water?" The crowd took up its chant: "Saltwater tea!" "Saltwater tea!" "Boston Harbor a teapot tonight!"

Unseen by many in the crowd, a small group of men in headdresses and painted faces, already waiting by the door, slipped out into the night.

Back at the tavern, the voices at the table were growing louder, as much, no doubt, from the effects of rum and ale as from the subjects being discussed. Still, Thompson Maxwell was concerned: The city, he knew, was full of Loyalist sympathizers, even spies, and all this talk of free trade was likely to turn some ears.

He said as much to Meade, who hastened to allay his fears.

"Thompson, Thompson, you fret far too much," said Meade, as he swung his arm around and pointed to the tavern owner. "Isaiah Wilcox, our proprietor, is a member of the Sons of Liberty. There's not a Tory in the city he can't pick of a crowd. He evens finds them sometimes"—Meade paused, and allowed himself a smile—"for the exchange of information that is, let us say, to our advantage to have them believe."

"What ever do you mean?"

"Why, just two days ago, Thompson, he let it be known that powder and muskets were on their way to Boston from the north, on the Cambridge Road"—he paused again, his eyes twinkling impishly.

"Oh, that was *your* route today, was it not?"

Thompson understood. He was incredulous. "No wonder—. . .

"You mean, no wonder Mr. Hancock seemed so unperturbed by your report of the loss of goods?"

"Yes."

"Indeed. We seldom enjoy such a firsthand account of our results."

Thompson smiled, then laughed out loud. He was impressed and thoroughly at ease for the first time today.

"Well, Mr. Meade, it sets my mind at ease that you and Mr. Hancock so well understand the reasons for my delay."

At precisely this moment, to Meade's left, a stranger approached John Right from behind. It was obvious that he had just come in from the cold; he was breathing heavily, from either excitement or exertion, or both. He leaned down, touched Right lightly on the shoulder, and spoke briefly into his ear. That done, he straightened, turned, and walked quickly from the room.

Right turned to address the group. His face was grave; all traces of levity were gone.

"Captain Rotch has returned. It is as expected. He had no success in convincing Governor Hutchinson to allow the *Dartmouth* safe passage with the tea."

It was Meade who spoke then.

"The governor knew our position. And he knew the deadline for unloading that ship was tomorrow. And still he quit Boston, to go to his country house. His contempt is clear. We must answer with our own."

"No more talking," said John Right. "We must leave. The crowd from the meeting is headed for Griffin's Wharf."

All six men rose at once.

"Put down your tankards, my friends," Right said. "Put on your dress. We Mohawks have work to do tonight."

5

GRIFFIN'S WHARF,
BOSTON HARBOR

GLANCING AROUND AS HE WALKED east toward the wharf with John Right, Thompson was amazed by the number of people in the streets. There had to be hundreds, perhaps a thousand, a new group at every corner. If so many citizens knew in advance of the evening's events, he wondered, how could it be that Governor Hutchinson and General Gage did not know as well?

Thompson was a stranger in Boston. If trouble developed with the British, there would be no one to whom he could turn. Except John Hancock—the last man in the city the governor would heed.

"What are we walking into?" he said to John Right. "My God, man, we are not even armed!"

Right smiled slightly and shook his head. His pace didn't slow.

"You need not worry. General Gage is in London and the governor is at his country house in Milton. The officer in charge will be slow to respond. Hutchinson won't know for hours."

"How is it you can be so certain? Suppose you're wrong?"

"There are sentinels on every corner, Sam Adams has seen to that, and on the docks and rooftops, too. Post riders will pass the word to the surrounding towns if the tea is unloaded. So if the garrison is mustered, we will be the first to know. If you hear the sound of tom-toms from the rooftops, strip off your feathers and melt into the crowd."

As they approached the foot of Pearl Street, they were joined by other small bands of Mohawks. From what Thompson could see, most of these "Indians" had used the same methods he and Hancock's men had—chicken feathers, and either stove ash or paint on their faces. John Right looked around, regarding the faces about him; he appeared satisfied.

Suddenly, without warning, he opened his mouth, took air deeply into his lungs, and let forth a curdling whoop. It was the sign. The assembled men split, efficiently, precisely, into two groups. Thompson, for all his military experience, could not help but be impressed. His own group, with him trailing, broke into a slow run, heading single file toward the wharf. Once there, they veered left without delay and, still running, still single file, boarded the *Dartmouth* by its main gangplank. The second group, one hundred feet to Thompson's right, boarded the *Eleanor* in the same fashion. The *Beaver,* warped alongside the others, would get the same treatment soon enough.

Aided by the bright moonlight and by lanterns held in the hands of a dozen or more men standing on the dock—Thompson had not even seen this group arrive—The Mohawks began their work. Many of the men, Thompson knew, had taken guard duty aboard the ships in recent weeks, so were familiar with them. He followed their lead across the decks. The custom officer of the *Dartmouth,* then of the *Eleanor,* was summarily forced off. Groups of men descended below, then reappeared—two men for every chest of tea. The chests were opened, smashed open with hatchets—sometimes several at once— hefted to the rails, then dumped. Thompson stood speechless, awed into paralysis by the efficiency of it all.

The rain of earlier in the day had abated; the night was crisp, cold, and clear. The hatchet chops sounded loud to Thompson's ears, although other than this the only sounds were the groaning of the ships and the slapping of the sea against their hulls.

"The tide is nearly out," said a sooty-faced man standing next to Thompson. Several Mohawks paused in their work to look over the side. Dark, heavy-looking mounds of tea bobbed in the water on all sides of the ship. "The tea is piling up," someone said.

"Jump in and clear it away!" joked a second.

For the next several minutes, using long poles and oars from the ship and the dock, the men worked to spread the clumps of tea. Then they went back to their dumping, pausing every ten minutes or so to spread the latest batch. It went on this way, without pause and almost without talking, for the next three hours, until the moon was high.

Thompson would learn later that the efforts of the men had been viewed by more than three thousand Boston citizens, as well as by the crews of other vessels moored nearby. Even Admiral Montague had seen it, Thompson was told, from the home of a Tory friend. Yet no one, of all these thousands, had seen fit to alert the English 64th and 65th regiments, who remained contentedly garrisoned on nearby Castle Island, ignorant to the end.

Every chest of tea, on all three ships, was emptied into the harbor. The shattered chests themselves were dumped overboard. Only then did the Mohawks depart, as quickly and quietly as they had arrived, stripping off feathers, wiping off paint, down the gangplanks and into the faceless crowd.

It was then, jumping in haste from the deck of the *Dartmouth*, that Thompson slipped. He felt something sharp gash his leg as he fell. He landed awkwardly, painfully. Embarrassed at his own clumsiness, he bit back the cry that formed in his throat and forced the pain from his mind.

But John Right, looking back, had seen him fall, and saw, for the briefest instant, the fire of pain in his eyes. He bent to examine the injured leg: "There is blood," he said, " but I think it is not severe. Might it be broken?"

Thompson shook his head, unable to speak.

"But painful, I think," Right said, quickly wrapping his own coat around the leg. He studied Thompson's face for an answer. There was none, only the smallest of nods.

Right called to two of the men who had been with him. "Quickly, carry him to the warehouse; we'll take care of him there." All three men together, as gently but as fast as they could, hoisted Thompson to his feet, then, in almost the same motion, forward and into the crowd.

Home of Joshua Atherton
The house, located just south of the village, remained intact until early in the twentieth century.

6

SEPTEMBER 20, 1774
AMHERST

JOSHUA FINISHED HIS NOON MEAL and walked into the sitting room.
Abigail, without so much as a glance in his direction, cleared the dishes off the table and strode outside to wash them. She scraped furiously at a plate, not noticing that there was nothing left to scrape.
Dishes clattered and utensils clanged against pots. She knew Joshua
would hear the din, and was glad.

She had rarely, if ever, felt so angry. Angry at being ignored—or at
least unheeded—in what she had begged for, in so many ways, so many,
many times: "Please, please, Joshua, for my sake, for our family's sake
if not for your own. Do not speak out so publicly. Please keep your
Loyalist sentiments to yourself. Why is that so very much to ask?"

And each time, however reluctantly, he had promised to try,
though his efforts, it seemed, never lasted longer than a week. And
each time, with each new incident, each overheard rumor, each dis-
approving look on the street, Abigail grew more angry, her patience
grew thinner, her anger took longer to abate.

But this time was the worst. Today, twice in an hour, she had seen
her darkest fears realized. First, a close neighbor had unmistakably
snubbed her. Then, as though to dispel all trace of doubt, a merchant

had refused her money, had refused to serve her in his store. "Why?" she had asked, nearly in tears, already knowing the answer. "Ask your husband, Mrs. Atherton," he had answered, and turned away.

"I'm sorry, Abigail. I'm sorry you were embarrassed on my account. I'll redouble my efforts to hold my tongue in public, but as I've told you and told you, it is most difficult sometimes." Those were his words exactly. Spoken calmly, almost coldly, at supper between mouthfuls of meat.

She had exploded as never before. Cried, screamed, ranted, wanted more than anything in the world to hurl a plate or a pot. But she did not. In the end, she had been measured and dutiful. She had wept quietly in her chair. And he, his noon meal finished, had risen slowly from the table and walked just as slowly out.

It was absurd, of course, this notion of her husband as the enemy, these rumors that he was, or "might be," an agent for the king. He was as loyal, she knew, as any man in Amherst, as loyal in his way as any Whig she knew. And he loved her, and loved their children, and would do nothing willfully to create peril for any of them.

All this she knew, and reminded herself for perhaps the hundredth time.

But it did nothing to dispel her anger, at the bottom of which, she had come to see, was fear–for her husband, for their family, for their peaceful, contented, prosperous way of life.

It was ironic, she thought: The very qualities she loved in him were those now driving her fears. Peaceful, honest, eloquent, fair but stubborn, incapable of hypocrisy, resistant to compromise. A practical idealist, that was her husband. She smiled for a second, in spite of herself.

And he might be right. That was what made it all so damnable. She knew, in her heart, that he might be right in the end: that the colonists, as a whole, did not want war with the crown; that they were overmatched in any event; that it was only the foolish zealotry of a handful–John Hancock, Sam Adams, Thompson Maxwell–that was heading them toward a war that would destroy their future, a war they couldn't win.

She wet her hands in the cold water and pressed them to her cheeks. She must gain control of herself and see to the rest of her duties. She would talk to her husband again later, when she had calmed herself further, when she had regained her strength.

She bent to retrieve a bucket from beside the well, then straightened as a movement caught her eye. There was dust rising in the distance, riders coming along the Post Road, six or eight of them, by the looks of it. She watched their approach, wondering distractedly what their business was, hoping she would not have to deal with visitors on such a difficult day.

Then she noticed, as they drew closer, that some of them were armed. The bucket flew from her hands, bouncing off the packed earth beside the well, as she ran for the house, calling for her husband.

Joshua jumped at the sound of Abigail's voice behind him. He had been staring out the window of their little sitting room, wondering what had become of the tranquillity of their lives.

"Joshua, there are riders coming! They're armed!"

There was naked fear in every syllable. He felt a flash of irritation, then a pang of guilt for being the cause. Looking past her out the window, he saw the riders. Their faces were close enough now to discern.

"Abigail, please. I'm sure it's nothing that can't be handled. No need for worry. I recognize at least one of them, Matthew Patten from Bedford. I dealt with him once in a boundary dispute. I believe you've met him–a justice of the peace and town clerk for Bedford. Does his name mean nothing to you?"

He was trying to calm her, and she knew it. But his words had no effect. Her cheeks remained flushed; her hair was rapidly escaping its careful knot. He almost smiled at the picture, but stopped himself. He took her hand instead. One of the riders was now dismounting. "See, it's Matthew Patten," he said.

Joshua didn't like the look on the men's faces. His mind flashed suddenly to an incident the previous month: Benjamin Whiting, the governor's agent from Hollis, had been beaten badly, in front of his home, by a group of angry Whigs. He steered his wife away from the window, then asked, as blandly as he could: "Abigail, would you get my fowling musket?" She said nothing, but left the room at his words. Somehow, oddly, she seemed to have regained her calm.

"Joshua! Joshua! I must speak with you." It was Matthew Patten, calling from the front step. Joshua approached the door.

Abigail was again at his side. Her arms were empty, folded resolutely in front of her. He looked at her and she returned his gaze. She had known, he thought, before he did, that the old fowling musket would be of no use against a band of armed men.

"Think of your family," she hissed as he pulled open the door and stepped onto the porch.

"What is your pleasure today, Mr. Patten?" If he could help it, he thought, he was not going to acknowledge the gravity of what he feared.

"A pleasure it is not, Squire Atherton. I have been summoned to fetch you and escort you to the courthouse."

Joshua was annoyed now; he felt his composure slip. Behind him, Abigail's silent tension burned like a brand.

"Escort me to the courthouse? Why? On whose orders? For what cause?"

"Joshua, I pray you, listen a moment. We have known each other many years. This is the reason the committee sent me. No harm is intended to you."

"Committee, what committee? On whose orders?"

As the exchange heated, two more men dismounted and approached. Patten waved them back.

"The Committee of Correspondence from the towns of Bedford, Hollis, Merrimack, and Goff Falls. They have met, and determined to hold an inquiry as to your loyalty." Patten looked openly miserable, as though he wished he could be anywhere else.

"We," he said, turning and waving an arm in the direction of the other riders, "we have been ordered by the committee to fetch you.

We have no alternative, Joshua. As a friend and colleague, I ask that you accompany me."

The futility of resistance was suddenly very clear. Joshua felt Abigail's hand on his arm, squeezing gently from behind. "If you would get my cloak, dear," he said.

"Joshua, Joshua, surely they cannot force you." His wife's voice was shrill. Her hand clutched his arm tighter, as though to pull him back toward the house.

"Mrs. Atherton," Patten said, gently, evenly, sensing her concern, "no harm will come to your husband. I did not wish to be involved with this inquiry. The committee insisted. And I thought it best, in the end, that he have a friend in attendance."

Abigail's eyes were slits. Patten finished lamely. "The assembly at the courthouse has an inquiry to make. Nothing more, I assure you. Your husband will be safe with us."

"What is this assembly and what does it want of Joshua?" Her voice was angry, but as strong and steady as her husband had ever heard it.

"There are over one hundred citizens waiting at the courthouse, all desiring to be assured of Squire Atherton's loyalty. Please, release him so that he might accompany us, and accept my assurances that he will not be harmed. If he does not come willingly, I fear the next meeting will convene here, at your home. Please, Mrs. Atherton"— Patten seemed to be pleading—"do not compel me to return alone."

Joshua turned to Abigail; her hands dropped limply to her sides. He held her gently by the shoulders and looked deep into her eyes.

"I think it best that I go with them."

"Joshua, I fear for us. I fear for the children."

"I as well, Abigail. It seems our colony, like Massachusetts, is determined to stumble blindly toward its own destruction by follow-ing the likes of those Boston troublemakers Hancock and Adams."

When Abigail returned with Joshua's cloak, Patten helped him on with it, then used the chance to take his old friend briefly aside: "I'll send the men on to the courthouse. They'll advise the assembly that you'll be arriving soon. Let us walk there together by way of Mack Hill, just you and I, Joshua, so I can talk with you alone."

"So long as you trust me not to overpower you and escape," Joshua muttered. He managed a wry smile. Patten's mouth remained closed and tight.

On their walk up Mack Hill to the courthouse, Matthew Patten described the dilemma in which he found himself. Much of it—most of it—was familiar to Joshua. Joshua appreciated, nonetheless, the man's sincerity, and couldn't help but feel sympathy for his plight.

"You are still respected, Joshua," said Patten, "among the citizens of Amherst, and none would seek to do you harm. Still, as an attorney, you have made enemies around the county—your profession is not held in the most positive light. Lawyers, as you surely know, mean an ill wind to some.

"And, of course, there is the matter of your sentiments, your outspokenness, on behalf of the king and crown."

Joshua said nothing, merely walked along musing, occasionally nodding his head.

"Be prepared, my friend," Patten cautioned him. "There will be a large group today. Most of the county will be represented in the room. You will not be harmed, I promise you, but more than that I cannot say. Much of the outcome, I should not need to tell you, will depend on you, on what you tell them, on your answers to the questions they pose."

Joshua stopped and turned to face his new adviser: "Thank you, Matthew. I should probably tell you, I have been expecting something like this. My friend Robert Means, the merchant, warned me that my views have traveled, apparently more widely than I might have supposed."

"It is a sensitive time, Joshua. Citizens are outraged. Especially now, with King George closing the port of Boston and the New

Hampshire Assembly being dissolved by the governor. We have two governments now—the king's through Governor Wentworth, who is now only a titular head of state, and the New Hampshire Provincial Congress formed by the people and now meeting in Exeter. If only Wentworth had allowed his assembly to establish a committee of correspondence and communicate with the other colonies, he would still have his own legislative body. But no, he had to dissolve the body. What choice did we have other than to form our own government?"

"I know, Matthew, but it's acts like that and the Boston Tea Party that have resulted in General Gage ordering the raid on the Massachusetts Provincial Powder House earlier this month. Further, he has threatened to remove the powder and arms stored in all towns in Massachusetts and New Hampshire. Without arms we will be helpless to defend ourselves, and we have expressed our anger. I heard that the day following the powder house raid there were more than four thousand armed patriots amassed on the Cambridge common. If it had not been for the wisdom of Joseph Warren, the men would have fired on any redcoat they encountered. This is frightening indeed."

"Joshua, please take my advice. For this one day, at least, and for the sake of your family, try to be that charming 'cloak orator' you know so well how to be. Most of those there today are expecting a show, a little sport, nothing more. Try to remember that. And for goodness' sake, don't lose your temper, no matter what happens."

Joshua sighed deeply, and again felt Abigail's desperate clutching on his arm.

"I accept your counsel, my friend. I will moderate my speech so as not to fan the flames. My wife is right. I must think of my family."

But for all the warnings, Joshua was taken aback by the sight of the crowd outside the courthouse. It was twice as large, at least, as the worst he had imagined, which meant, he knew, that the inside of the building must be packed with men as well. Fortunately, none appeared to be in an angry mood, and he received a not unfriendly nod here and there.

Inside the courthouse, the Committee of Inquisition was in place, sitting in chairs around a table in front of the judge's bench. Captain Hildreth, proprietor of Jones Tavern, appeared to be in charge. Coldly but politely, Hildreth introduced the panel of five inquisitors to Joshua, who knew only three of the men: Hildreth himself, Matthew Patten, and Col. John Shepard, an Amherst neighbor with whom he had several times done business.

"Squire Atherton," Captain Hildredth began, rising from his chair behind the judge's bench, "we called this inquisition at the request of members of the Committee of Correspondence from the surrounding towns, the reason being that it has been widely reported that you have sworn allegiance to the king and to Governor Wentworth, rather than to your fellow citizens. Further, you have spoken out in condemnation of those patriots who have argued that, as New Hampshire citizens, we should have the freedom to choose our own future."

Hildreth's voice was that of a true tavern keeper, its natural volume and intensity made to carry across a crowded and noisy barroom. Having spoken, he paused briefly to allow the muttering of the assembly to subside, then said sharply: "Your loyalty is in question. We must know your sympathies. Are you, for instance, as it has been reported, a spy in allegiance with the king?"

Joshua drew in a deep breath. Things were moving from fact into rumor—the wrong word, a word wrongly spoken, could inflame some passions. He would need to tread carefully. Eloquence, persuasiveness, a measure of charm–they were tradable commodities now. The truth meant less to some than to others, especially when heated up by a cause. He sensed that the wrong word or attitude could inflame some of the ruffians present, mean-spirited men who flocked to occasions like this solely for sport and the hope of a fight. Eloquence, persuasiveness, and very great care were needed today.

Turning to Captain Hildreth and the inquisitors, Atherton spoke in a voice that could be heard only by a few. "Captain Hildreth, you and others in this room have known me for years. You know my honesty, my frankness. You know, also, that while we may not always agree, the freedom to speak one's mind is vital in a free society—so vital, in fact, that many men here would gladly risk their lives in its name.

"I know that I have been the subject of a sea of rumors, some true, most not. I ask only that you to be specific, so that I might know what to respond."

There was general unrest among the assembly. The noise of conflicting voices filled the hall: "Tory! Tory! He's a spy for the king!" "Let him talk! Let the man have his say!" "The time for talking is done! Let's teach him a lesson he'll not soon forget!"

The boom of Captain Hildreth's voice, like a gunshot, quelled the din: "I know most of you, if not by name, then by sight. I cannot throw you out of the public meetinghouse, but by God! If you expect hospitality in my establishment an hour from now, I advise you to be civil in the meeting I am doing my best to run!"

That was all it took. The noise quieted, almost instantly, to an intermittent muttering. Captain Hildreth nodded, clearly pleased with himself, then went on:

"Squire Atherton, your request is reasonable. Yes, you have been a favorite target in the county—even, I would say, the most popular dish in the skillet these days."

There was some quiet laughter. Hildreth had established the order he wanted, and was now setting the tenor of things: "We have two affidavits, Squire Atherton. The first is from Thompson Maxwell, the second from the Honorable Judge Wyseman Claggett. My intention is to read both, then to allow you to answer. Each addresses the issue of your loyalty to America and to New Hampshire. Are you prepared to hear these readings, sir?"

Joshua, standing as straight as he could, nodded that he was.

"The first, from Mr. Maxwell, reads as follows: 'I, Thompson

Maxwell, of Amherst, was riding by a group of Amherst citizens in front of the Means mansion when I heard Squire Atherton exclaim in a loud voice that men such as John Hancock, John Adams, and the other Sons of Liberty in Boston would do us no good, but rather have us under the guns of British soldiers, and the liberty we now possess will be lost. He said that in his opinion the damn rebels should suffer the king's gallows.'

"'Sworn before me, Jonas Dix, Justice of the Peace, on August 30, 1774.'"

The noise in the courthouse swelled dangerously. Captain Hildreth glared at the company, silenced them with a look, then raised his voice once again:

"The second affidavit, Squire Atherton, is from the Honorable Judge Wyseman Claggett. Judge Claggett states: 'I Wyseman Claggett, Judge, Justice of the Peace of Litchfield, state that in my presence on September 10 of this year, Attorney Joshua Atherton was before me in County Court. While in a conversation with me and other loyal patriots, he did emphatically state that he approved of the acts of General Gage in raiding the powder and arms of the colonies. He stated that in his opinion this was the proper course to stop armed resistance against the king.'

"'Sworn before me, Jonas Dix, Justice of the Peace, on September 15, 1774.'"

The din in the courtroom rose to a new peak. Captain Hildreth banged his gavel, almost violently, on the bench. The roar desisted. Hildreth turned to Joshua:

"Joshua Atherton, how say you to these statements?"

Joshua rose. He looked first at Captain Hildreth, then, individually, at each of the inquisitors on the bench. That done, he turned to the assembled group. He knew that deportment, humility, and eloquence were the key. The assembly was dangerously close to getting out of hand, and he knew that Captain Hildreth could do little if the crowd became a mob. It was up to him. Joshua had learned early in his practice of law that a sense of theater was important, and if a lawyer was to be successful, he must establish a presence to set him off from the other lawyers. It was his long black cloak that established his courtroom identity. Quietly, for a moment, he stared out at the faces in front of him. Then he reached down to the hem of his cloak and swept it, with a flourish, over his opposite shoulder. It was the "cloak orator" pose. Swaying slightly, almost hypnotically, he looked out to the farthest corner of the room, slowly gathered his thoughts, then began to speak:

"Captain Hildreth, citizens! Some of you know me personally, others by reputation. However you came to your knowledge, you know I will not lie. That said, let me first address the subject that is the reason for our being here today—loyalty. Let me speak to you of loyalty, my friends.

"First and absolute we have our loyalty God. It is to God we must answer in the end.

"Second only to God is my loyalty to America and to New Hampshire. I, as all of you, have been given the gift of this land, *our* land, the source of our prosperity, the future for our children, and for their children after that. It is my future, my young son Charles's future, the future for children as yet unborn."

He stopped. Looking over the group, still swaying slightly, his cloak still wrapped around him, he cast his eyes about, pausing momentarily at every face he thought he might know. He continued: "Yes, I am loyal. I am as loyal as any of you. I want, for my family, for myself, what you want for you and yours. We share the same future in this great land. Consider what a life we would have if we were now living in England—few are as free or as prosperous as we . . . "

The room began to stir again. Boredom was setting in. "Answer the affidavits!" came a voice from the back. "Answer the charges!" cried another. "Are you a spy for the king?"

Joshua drew a deep breath, then set his jaw for what now was the only course that remained. When he resumed, it was with fresh resolve: "Do I believe Adams and Hancock are taking the wrong course? Yes, I do, but this makes me no less loyal than you. The words were spoken in anger, but I do believe that a peaceful course is best. The king and his army are too powerful for us; we should negotiate with England, not oppose it in war.

"As for my exchange with Judge Claggett, yes, I recall speaking with him, but no, I do not recall that the words in that affidavit were spoken by me. Bear in mind, if you will, the phrase, 'I'll Claggett you.' If you have ever had cause to do business with the judge, you know what it means. If trouble is to be stirred up, it is not I but the judge who will stir it. Is there a man present who would dispute that?"

Joshua paused and looked around. He was ready for what he hoped would be his closing words: "Captain Hildreth, if you please. Allow me to swear my loyalty, before all of you, under oath."

Hildreth looked pleased. He picked up a paper that lay ready before him and stood to address the assembly. "Squire Atherton, the committee has prepared the following document. With your permission, I will read it aloud. Following my reading, I would pray you sign it, so this matter can be closed."

"Read on, sir."

Hildreth drew himself up to his full height and read the words with all the solemnity of a judge: "Whereas, I, Joshua Atherton, have, over a period of time, both done and said many things that I am sensible have proved of great disadvantage to this town, and to the colonies in general, I am now determined by my future conduct to convince the public that I will risk my life and interest in defense of the constitutional privileges of this continent, and humbly ask the forgiveness of my friends and the country in general for my past conduct."

He handed the paper to Joshua. "Squire Atherton, would you put your name to this document, so that all present can be assured of your loyalty?"

"Yes, I will be honored to do so, sir.

Joshua signed his name. There was a measured silence in the room. Then he spoke again. This time he was smiling, for the first time all day.

"Captain Hildreth," Joshua said, "will you do me the honor of treating my colleagues here to the hospitality of Jones Tavern? Flip, toddy punch, or rum, at my expense."

The silence continued for a moment, then was broken by the innkeeper's words: "You have heard Squire Atherton, our friend and patriot. What say you now?"

The assembly broke into cheers. There were cries of "Well done, well done!" and "To the tavern!" The doors in the back flew open; a hundred citizens surged forward, each man now intent on the latest mission of the day—to be the first across Jones Road.

Kendall House and Store

The southern half of the house was constructed in 1750; the northern portion was moved from a location south of the village and attached. In this location Nathan Kendall lived and operated his general store. The small building that housed the store was moved to the corner of Mack Hill and Jones Road in the nineteenth century.

7

OCTOBER 1774
AMHERST, THE HARVEST BALL

It had been a month since Joshua's day of vindication. Abigail was making her final preparations for the party at the Kendall house, the premiere event of the year. She was excited; it was the first such occasion to which the Athertons had been invited in longer than she could recall.

The whispering had ended. In town, the merchants once again smiled and welcomed her business; there were no more averted faces in the street. Joshua's business, after a lull, was again prospering. The town, if it had not exactly forgotten, seemed more than prepared to forgive, which, Abigail suspected, probably explained why Mary Means and Rebecca Kendall had invited her to join them in preparations for the ball.

"Abigail, Abigail," came the call from downstairs. "Are you ready? We are late as it is. We must leave now if we're not to embarrass ourselves."

"I am almost dressed. Only a moment more."

"If you had not spent most of the day at the Kendall house, we would be there by now, in time to greet the guests. And I"—her husband chuckled, a short laugh that was not meant to escape her—"I would not have had to spend three hours tending the fire and delivering your chine of pork that now sits, I would remind you, dear lady, on the Kendalls' table, while we, its source and inspiration, remain here."

Abigail laughed out loud. "Oh, yes! Oh, yes! Sitting beside the Kendalls' haunch of venison, not to mention the three roast turkeys delivered by the Meanses—are you telling me that was such a hardship? Or is it only that you fear they'll be devoured before you arrive?"

"I am concerned only with the wishes of our hosts," Joshua answered in mock dignity, as his wife descended the stairs.

They both laughed. Joshua's preoccupation with food was a running joke, although until recently the jokes—about food or about anything else—had been few and far between.

"May I say, madam, that you yourself will be a most charming asset to the ball this evening?" Joshua took his wife's hand with a courtly gesture. Abigail blushed and waved him off, but not without a smile.

"You said we would be late, Joshua. So then, let's be on our way!"

As they drove their horse cart up Mack Hill toward the Meanses', Abigail was gentle with her husband: "I expect you will be pleased with the delicacies prepared for the evening. I ask only two things of you. The first is, please, Joshua, be moderate in your consumption; you know you have a tendency to overindulge."

"And what is the second? For I sense you have the saved the larger request for last."

"First, Joshua, you must promise me you will abide by my wishes. It is more than a request—it is the most earnest plea I could ask."

Joshua knew the tone of his wife's voice well enough not to make light of her words. He had a sense of what was coming. "All right, I promise," he said.

"Joshua, I am not asking anything of you that all of the ladies on the committee are not asking of their husbands. There are dark clouds building. Horrible clouds. Clouds that might divide us. This, tonight, the Harvest Ball, it could be the last time all of us, Whigs and Tories, those who support Sam Adams and those who support the king, can be together as neighbors, as friends. Please, Joshua, I pray you, say nothing, do nothing, to stand in the way of our festiveness tonight."

Joshua was quiet, realizing the importance of the moment. It was not often his wife put her needs so nakedly on view.

"No, Abigail," he said finally. "You will see. All this will pass. The king will moderate his views."

"Not everyone agrees with you, Joshua. But whoever may be right, my entreaty remains the same. "Please, no discussions of politics this evening. Not a *mention* of Whigs or Tories, or taxes or the king. Please, Joshua, none at all!"

The Kendall house was in sight. Scores of carriages, horses, and wagons filled the road and the field next to the house. It was sure to be a grand evening, thought Joshua; his wife had not looked forward to anything this much in as long as he could recall. He would not compromise it for her.

"I promise, Abigail."

It was just twilight, and already the lanterns and candles had been lit. The outlines of gaily dressed men and women could be seen passing by the windows as they walked from room to room. An addition to the house, not yet completed, was far enough along, thought Joshua, to make it the perfect choice for this year's Harvest Ball. Next to the Meanses' mansion and the Dana home, the Kendalls' was easily the largest house in town.

The new hall, he noted, had been enlarged; the stairway was now wide enough to allow couples, even women in hoop skirts, to ascend comfortably side by side. The second floor had been turned into a ballroom. At one corner, a quartet of fiddlers played a harvest tune. Candles and lanterns were everywhere, illuminating the throng in their party finery, moving in waves from room to room. All in all, thought Joshua, the scene was a vivid tribute to the success of the Kendalls' store.

Following a brief tour of the house, Abigail departed for her duties as co-host. Joshua, in her absence, wandered toward the dining room, where he was met at the door by Captain Hildreth, who was deep in conversation with the Reverend Mr. Wilkins and a third man he did not know. For the briefest moment, Joshua's mind flashed back to his talk with the minister six months before, on their way back from the opening of spring court. It seemed already years ago.

"An adequate repast, is it not, Joshua?" remarked Captain Hildreth, plucking a codfish ball from the table and starting to chew.

"Yes," replied Joshua, "and I am certain that, together, the several of us could make an educated assessment as to which Amherst household is the source of any dish here."

So for the next several minutes, joined by Daniel Campbell and Robert Read, the men played at this game: assigning every dish at the banquet—roast goose, onions and cream, pork and beans, brown bread, boiled parsley potatoes, buttermilk biscuits, corn pudding—to the family they believed had brought it. There was general agreement on most dishes, though no consensus on the source of the cold tongue or the red beet eggs. Abigail's chine of pork, by every estimate but her husband's (he remained neutral on the matter), was named the favorite offering of the night.

"The way the guests are attacking it," the minister commented, "you would think it was a company of British regulars."

"Ah-ah, Mr. Wilkins," Joshua taunted him, waving an accusing finger teasingly in his face, "clearly you have not been instructed as to the evening's decorum. None of us, per order of the ladies, shall make any political reference, however small or good-natured. The ladies—my wife especially, I suspect—are eager to avoid any appearance of discord among the guests."

The minister laughed. "Your wife, I think, is a most sensible woman. We would all be well advised to heed her counsel."

It took him some time in the swell of people, but Joshua finally located Abigail, talking with a group of friends in the parlor.

"There you are," he said, and took her elbow gently. "If you ladies will excuse my wife, I promised her a dance before I consume so much of these magnificent offerings that I am unable to move."

As they climbed the stairway side by side, Abigail jabbed her elbow lightly into her husband's ribs. "You are fortunate that most of those present are familiar with your sense of humor," she said. "When it combines with your natural honesty, it could be embarrassing to you if we were not in the company of friends."

As they reached the top of the stairs and glanced about, they were surprised at the number of couples they knew. Robert and Mary Means were talking to Moses Kelly, the new sheriff of Hillsborough County. Sheriff Kelly, Joshua saw, was gesturing in the direction of Zaccheus Cutler, another storekeeper from Amherst, who had been standing by the doorway, apparently listening to the fiddlers. As Joshua passed by, he overheard the sheriff, making little effort to guard his words: "That damnable Tory. What is *he* doing here tonight?"

Robert Means—to his credit, Joshua thought—replied instantly, with only the thinnest veil of courtesy in his voice: "He is here as our guest, as you are. You would do well to recall that, Sheriff. This may be our last chance for a cordial occasion among friends for some time, if events keep on as they are."

Mary Means, the hostess, abruptly cut short the discussion. "Sheriff Kelly, would you care to accompany me to the dance floor? Robert has no taste for dancing, I'm afraid."

Robert Means hailed the Athertons as they approached.

"What a glorious home the Kendalls have. Ideal for an event such as this. I should perhaps consider an expansion of my own home, as the plain is now the new center of town. As for you, Joshua, soon you'll not need to travel up Mack Hill to the county courthouse to get to work in the morning."

Joshua nodded and smiled, then placed a hand lightly on Robert Means's arm.

"Robert, would you kindly keep Abigail company for a moment? I'm sure Zaccheus overheard what the sheriff just had to say. I want to assure him that he doesn't speak for all of us here."

Zaccheus was walking down the stairs when Joshua caught up to him.

"Joshua, a kindred spirit at last!" his friend said in a jovial tone, not quite succeeding in concealing his hurt. "It's good to see you. You're looking very well."

"Yourself as well," Joshua answered. "Zaccheus, I want to assure you that we welcome you here and wish that you will remain. You are a friend to all of us. Sheriff Kelly was only flexing his new muscles a bit. I am surprised, frankly, that he was appointed to the post, considering the outspokenness of his views. He must have an excellent friend in the governor."

"It matters little to me, Joshua. I plan to leave for Boston shortly, to join General Gage. I've heard he's accepting colonial volunteers. Colonel Stark's nephew, did you know, has just accepted a commission in the king's army."

Although Zaccheus's voice was not loud, Joshua motioned him to be cautious. Couples were passing on the stairway; this was not apt to be popular talk.

"If you leave, Zaccheus, you will be abandoning your house, your property, all that you worked so hard to earn. Unfortunately, with the new laws, you may never be permitted to return."

"Joshua, you and I believe the same, that the colonies cannot possibly prevail. King George is sending more soldiers by the month; General Gage is raiding our powder supplies. You yourself, if you remain too long, will suffer the same fate as the Tories we have heard about in Massachusetts and Connecticut. You would look rather silly in tar and feathers, my friend."

Zaccheus looked worn out. Joshua understood all too well, and felt a wave of sudden sympathy for the younger man.

"I believe it will not come to that in New Hampshire. We have too much respect for our neighbors to put them through such things. And in any case"—he laughed ruefully, patting his stomach—"I could never survive the rigors of army life. Aside from my girth, my health has never been the best. My father always hoped I'd be a farmer, and I was not even able to manage the trials of that. As a soldier, I fear, I would be a total loss."

"You do yourself a disservice, Joshua. And I think where these troubles are concerned, you have too much faith in your fellow man. Why, just look at what you underwent last month, being hauled before the committee and made to explain yourself. It could happen again, and with less friendly results."

They said their farewells, and Joshua felt a weight settle on his heart as he watched Zaccheus walk out the door. He sensed this would be their last meeting. He had known Zaccheus Cutler many years, even before his move to Amherst, and was saddened to think that he might not see his friend again. His mood turned suddenly melancholy. There were too many friends, he thought, even family members, becoming divided and apart. And for what? For what?

Making his way through the groups of guests, occasionally stopping to greet this or that friend, he found himself back in the ballroom, where Abigail and Robert Means were congratulating Paul Dudley Sargent on his appointment as a delegate to the New Hampshire Provincial Congress. Held in Exeter, the congress had been formed as the citizens' government, in direct contravention of the governor's orders, in brazen defiance of the crown.

Sargent was describing what he termed Governor Wentworth's "incredulousness" at the congress's new independence: "He calls us 'lawless.' We are not lawless, it is only that the laws we follow now are not his. If he had allowed his assembly to form a Committee of Correspondence in the first place, so we could stay in touch with the

Amherst Powder House

As a secure site to store the town's supply of ammunition, the building was constructed of chestnut logs, twelve inches thick and plastered on the outside. The structure was removed in the mid-nineteenth century.

other colonies, he would still have his assembly. But no, he feared that too much. So what was the result? Now he has no effective government at all."

Joshua stood to one side, shaking his head. For several minutes he kept his silence. Finally, as Sargent's words grew more voluble, he could hold his tongue no more: "Paul, I am sorry, but I am afraid I cannot agree with you, or with the new appointment you have. It will do nothing but inflame passions further. It will do nothing but divide people more."

Abigail's elbow was once again in his ribs, much more sharply this time. He threw her a contrite look, and they excused themselves. As he guided her toward an open section of the dance floor, he was suddenly bumped from one side; turning instinctively to apologize for not looking where he was going, he found himself face to face with Sheriff Kelly, whose breath smelled strongly of rum.

"Did you have a nice talk with your friend Zaccheus Cutler, Attorney Atherton? Rumor has it he will not be with us for long."

Abigail looked from one man to the other, bewildered. Joshua did not like the sheriff's tone, and made no effort to hide his disdain. "I do not listen to rumor, Sheriff. I have better things to occupy my time."

Abigail gave a little gasp of surprise as he took her arm firmly and swept her onto the dance floor.

8

DECEMBER 22, 1774
AMHERST

THE NIGHT WAS WET AND RAW, and Thompson Maxwell was restless. The hour was late. His leg injury of a year ago, though not serious, ached as it tended to do in damp weather. Quietly, so as not to awaken Sybel, he eased from his bed and descended the stairs to the kitchen. He sat in Sybel's rocking chair in front of the coals glowing in the fireplace and massaged his leg. The throbbing took him back a year ago to Boston and to his clumsiness.

John Hancock himself had inspected the wound, after Thompson had been returned to the warehouse from Griffin's Wharf that night. Still feeling a fool for having made himself the center of attention at such a critical point, he lay quietly, determined not to complain. Hancock ordered the cut bound and Thompson's wagon made ready for departure, then assigned one of his own men to drive it, insisting that Thompson needed rest and that he return to New Hampshire right away.

"There were too many witnesses," Hancock said. "When Hutchinson hears of the tea-dumping, he will stop at nothing to find out who was involved. Your wound will be remembered, and would cause you to stand out. We must get you out of Boston as soon as possible."

Thompson had protested. "But Mr. Hancock, my brother-in-law lives in Bedford, Massachusetts. Surely I can stay there, and he can care for me."

"No, Mr. Maxwell, the farther from Boston, the better. You'd do best back in Amherst. We will load your wagon and get you started by early morning. Now get some rest."

Thompson had been well cared for—cosseted, really—by his aunt and uncle in Amherst village, closer to medical care than at his farm. His militia friends helped Sybel with the farm chores until he healed. Uncle Ned was delighted to have him a captive; he was hungry for any news from Boston, and pumped his nephew constantly until called off finally by his wife. Thompson, for his part, offered his accounts willingly until, at the end of a week, when he was feeling well enough to limp around, Uncle Ned asked if he would be willing to share them at a selectmen's meeting.

Thompson smiled now at the memory. Wrapped in a blanket, with a cup of rum, lemon, and hot water on the table beside him, he recalled his uncle's eager overtures that night. All he had wanted to do was to doze in Aunt Hannah's warm kitchen after a dinner of corn pudding and beef. But his uncle had insisted—"It will do you good to use the leg"—then had left to saddle the horses without waiting for his nephew to protest.

The meetinghouse stood a distance up Mack Hill from Uncle Ned's farm, at the junction of Mack Hill and Jones Road. The first ever built in Amherst, it had stood at this location since 1739. Still unfinished on the outside, at forty-five feet long by twenty-two feet wide, with a ceiling height of twenty feet, it was an adequate size for town affairs and for use as the Congregational church. But later, after Amherst was named the county seat—with a requirement now for courthouse space—some of the newer members of the congregation had found themselves relegated to sitting in pews just outside the front door or in pews constructed under the rafters.

Much as he had anticipated, Thompson's leg was throbbing badly by the time they reached the meetinghouse, which was not discernibly warmer than the air outside. The selectmen, his uncle had told him, didn't approve of a heated building and refused to fund the purchase of a stove. "The colder the meetinghouse, the shorter the meeting" was the popular rationale.

Thompson was confused as to the purpose of his presence. The meeting didn't seem to concern the Amherst militia; the most important order of business was a complaint from a farmer on Mack Hill who was losing his sheep to wolves. The selectmen said they would take the matter "under advisement"; the farmer left muttering unhappily, suspecting correctly that his sheep remained at risk. The chairman of the building committee reported on the dedication of the second meetinghouse, to take place the following month. Thompson had been present at the raising, and had helped with his oxen to move and raise the heavy beams. Still, from the descriptions he was hearing, shamelessly embellished, the event sounded nothing at all like the one he recalled

The selectmen were nostalgic. This was to be the last meeting in the original building since the raising of the frame of the new meetinghouse more than a year ago. Finally the building was ready for occupancy. But tonight the men took their time, relishing their memories of this building that had served the town so ably for twenty-five years. At last the meeting ended, and Thompson was more than ready to start the journey home.

"Why don't we stop by Jones Tavern, it's early yet."

It was his uncle speaking, with three selectmen and the chairman of the building committee enthusiastically adding their votes. There was nothing Thompson could say; he went along with as much grace as he could muster, thinking that the tavern, at least, would be warm.

Entering, they found a table with ease, ordered their drinks, and settled in. It was only then that Thompson understood why Uncle Ned had wanted him along.

"Let my nephew tell you of his adventures at the tea party in Boston Harbor," said Ned. "Tell them, Thompson, how it was you injured your leg."

"Do you mean that I nearly froze to death tonight, with my leg throbbing all evening, only so you could hear again my news of John Hancock and the rest?"

"Ah, but it's not for me," Uncle Ned protested with a smile. "I have heard the story myself, to be sure, but these men here are members of the Committee of Correspondence. It is important they understand such events from the mouth of one who was there!"

Thompson sighed, took a long swallow from his glass of rum, and began his tale anew.

The next he knew, there was a knock at the door, and he was startled from his slumber back to the present. Two sharp raps, then two more, then half a dozen in quick succession. Thompson groaned and opened his eyes. His head hurt, his back ached. The darkness of the room, with the fire nearly extinguished, was too thick for his eyes to penetrate. The knocking continued, louder, and he remembered where he was.

He rose from the table, his legs barely supporting him, and shuffled to the door.

"Who is it?"

"Private Robinson, sir. Private Peter Robinson. Captain Crosby sent me to fetch you."

Thompson pulled open the door. A shivering, wet-haired young soldier stared back at him. It was not a night to be out. A coating of wet snow had long since turned to slush, and the young private was soaked to the skin. Thompson beckoned him in.

"No, sir, thank you, sir," came the reply. "Captain Crosby has sent me to request all officers to assemble at the meetinghouse at seven in the morning. A rider has arrived from Portsmouth. The Hillsborough County Committee of Safety and officers from the militia companies are to meet to hear the news of the raid on Fort William and Mary this past week. I would gladly come in and dry off, sir, but I am only halfway through my stops."

Thompson attempted to inquire further, but Private Robinson abruptly turned back into the sleet, mounted his horse, and rode off.

Two hours later, arriving at the meetinghouse, Thompson saw that officers from all three of Amherst's militia companies were present, as well as at least twenty men he did not know. He noticed, too, that all present were in small groups, talking to one another. He surmised that each group was a separate militia unit. The only thing the men seemed to have in common was their wet hair and clothes.

Around 7:30, Captain Crosby closed the outside door and ordered Private Robinson to admit no one else. Paul Dudley Sargent, the chairman of the county Committee of Safety, took the podium and asked that the militia commanders from each town introduce their officers. This done, he bade everyone to take a seat. When the room had quieted, Sargent spoke once more: "The first shots have been fired. And in New Hampshire, at Portsmouth. This may be the beginning."

The reactions in the room were mixed. Some of the men cheered; others groaned; still others sat stunned. Rapping his cane twice on the podium, Sargent called for silence. "Time is short for our guest," he told the crowd. "He has other towns to ride to. For his own safety, I will not give his name. Suffice it to say, he is a member of the Committee of Safety in Exeter. Listen closely, I pray you, to his words."

With that, Sargent gestured to a man sitting quietly at the perimeter of the gathering. The gentleman rose, walked to the podium, and stood next to the chairman. He was well in excess of six feet tall, slender, bearded, roughly thirty-five years old. Greeting the room with a single two-armed wave, he began his announcement: "Looking outside at the miserable weather, you might think it not such a good day. But no. It is a glorious day. On this day, my friends, may well begin our ultimate severance from the crown!"

He stopped for a moment, looked around the room briefly, then continued:

"Gentlemen, on the thirteenth of this month we received a messenger from Boston. Paul Revere delivered news from the Sons of Liberty that General Gage had received orders to confiscate the stores of powder and weapons in and around Massachusetts."

The room erupted in a cacophony of disjointed chants: "He can't do that!" "That powder is *ours*!" "We need those supplies for *protection*!"

The speaker continued his summary of events. He related how, on December 14, one day following Paul Revere's delivery of the news, four hundred militiamen had marched through the streets of Portsmouth to the home of Governor Wentworth, where they had demanded to know the truth; how the governor had at first refused to answer, then had admitted that General Gage was imposing an embargo on all gunpowder and arms to the countryside. "He knows that without weapons our cause will be lost. He has already raided powder houses near Boston."

Once again the assembly turned raucous, and Sargent seemed in danger of losing control.

"Is this rumor or fact? I've heard too much false news from Boston!" someone shouted.

"What do you propose we do?" another called out.

The speaker spread his hands to the group, as though to ask for calm. Then he smiled—a little slyly, Thompson Maxwell thought— and continued: "Ah, but the tale does not end there. The entire mob, all four hundred of us, marched on Fort William and Mary, which we found to be guarded by only a single officer and five enlisted men."

There was a series of small gasps, then the room fell silent.

"Capt. Thomas Pickering and Maj. John Langdon demanded that the fort be surrendered. The British officer drew his sword, ordering us to disperse."

From the rear of the meetinghouse, there were the sounds of muffled laughter.

"After a volley of shots, one of the redcoats was wounded, and he surrendered the fort. In a couple of hours, we moved more than one hundred barrels of powder and a large quantity of firearms. The next day, Governor Wentworth—"

"That Tory bastard," Thompson heard a man in front of him mutter.

"—called a public meeting of the officials in Portsmouth and demanded the return of the fort and munitions and the arrest of those responsible. The assembly dispersed quietly. I am quite certain the governor left thinking his conditions would be met. They were not, of course."

By now, the laughter was general throughout the room.

"One of our brethren, Maj. John Sullivan of Durham, was so inflamed by the governor's sanctimony that he led his men from the Durham militia to the fort that very night and removed sixteen cannon, approximately sixty muskets, and more powder. All have since been distributed to the surrounding towns for safekeeping."

"Three cheers for Durham!" "Just desserts for the governor!"

"The message I bring you, and to the towns farther west, is to do as we have done in Portsmouth. Gather supplies with haste, maintain your arsenal in safe locations. There will be a need."

Everyone began talking at once. Sargent pounded the gavel once, with more force than Thompson had thought he possessed. "This meeting is ended," Sargent said. "Pass the word to all those you meet—the first shots have been fired. And in New Hampshire!"

9

APRIL 15, 1775
PROVINCE HOUSE, BOSTON

HALFWAY UP THE STEPS TO THE FRONT DOOR of Province House, Maj. John Pitcarin heard a loud slam directly above his head. Looking up, he was just in time to miss colliding with General Gage's wife, Margaret, her skirt flying behind her, on her way down the same set of stairs. He opened his mouth for a greeting, but she was by him in a blur, nearly flattening him against the railing as she passed. Seconds later, she was into her waiting carriage and gone.

Pitcarin gazed after her. He had known Margaret Gage for a number of years; her moods no longer surprised him. A strong-minded woman, especially when it came to the cause of colonial liberty—which she believed in with a passion that would not allow for compromise—she was suspected by some officers of being a confederate of the patriots, even of being the source of some recent sensitive leaks.

Pitcarin would never have said so, but he would not be surprised if there were some truth to all this. Mrs. Gage made no secret of her opinions; it was not unusual for her to lecture dinner guests on the subject of "liberty" and "justice" for her native colonies. As rich and beautiful as she was, the major had recently confided to a friend, "General Gage has far more patience than I."

As he came through the front doors, the first sight that greeted

Province House in Boston
Headquarters for Governor and General Thomas Gage
until the evacuation of Boston on March 17, 1776.

Pitcarin was the general: in the entranceway to his office, red-faced and breathing heavily. For a moment, he appeared almost unaware of his surroundings. The major waited dutifully. In time, the general nodded, smiled thinly, and beckoned him in.

Thomas Gage looked at least ten years older than his forty-four years. He was overweight, mostly bald, and pale-complecated, with the tired, haunted look of a man on whom the world weighed heavily indeed.

"I apologize for Margaret's behavior just now. I love her dearly, but she can be a most exasperating woman. She is angry with me, of course. I suggested that some information from this headquarters had somehow found its way to a meeting of the Sons of Liberty. She became emotional, insisting I was accusing her of being a spy."

Pitcarin could only stand and stare: the commander of the king's army in the colonies, disconsolate over an exchange with his wife. He was considering his response—something safe, he thought, some small platitude that risked nothing—when an outburst from the general chased all further thoughts from his mind.

"Damn this city! Damn the entire colony! Nothing is secret! It's like trying to hold water in a bucket without a bottom!"

He paced the floor behind his desk, shaking his head, saying nothing. When he spoke again, he had collected himself.

There was a knock at the door. Lt. Col. Francis Smith, possibly the most corpulent officer in the British army, was ushered into the room by an aide. Gage waited until the door was once again closed, then requested the two officers to join him at the table. Pitcarin watched, hiding his amusement, as Smith slowly eased his bulk into a chair.

For the next several minutes, the three men discussed the problem before them. For almost four months now, since the raid on Fort William and Mary at New Castle, adjoining Portsmouth, in December, the colonists, with ever greater impunity, had been sacking British garrisons and stealing munitions. Even more galling, colonial militia units in Massachusetts, Connecticut, and New Hampshire were now offering bribes of money and land as enticement to British regulars, who would then train the American militia in the latest British military techniques. The news of all this reached London. It was this that the general had summoned the men to report: "The king—and Parliament as well, I am told—feels that I have been too patient. I have been ordered, accordingly, to arrest and send the leaders back to England, and also, to stop the importation of gunpowder, by whatever means possible. And to find and confiscate the colonies' munitions and supplies."

Privately, Pitcarin agreed with this directive, though the irony was hard to escape: The British army was forced to disarm the militia system it had mandated and supplied only decades earlier. That, of course, had been for the defense of the colonies against the Indians and French. Now the rebels, more emboldened, possessed not only those arms, but also the large caches they were stealing daily from the crown.

"It's time we put the fear of God into the rascals," put in Colonel Smith. "From my experience with them, they talk a good game, but are quick to run from anything more serious than a turkey hunt. They will be helpless if we disarm them. Let them talk, preach, and rally all they like. Without weapons, and with us controlling the coast and the Indians at their backs, there will be nothing they can do."

The wattles on the colonel's chin bobbed up and down as he talked. He leaned back in his chair, pleased with himself

"Yes, Colonel Smith," Gage responded, with only barely concealed impatience. "But unless we capture their leaders, they may secure replacement arms from the French. Adams, Hancock, Paine, Franklin—they're already in touch with the French government. We have that on good authority."

Gage said nothing for a moment, then leaned forward, elbows on the table, both hands under his chin. He looked from one to the other and nodded.

"Yes, the king is right. We must round up the leaders. And we must do so at once."

Taking a seat at the table, the general went on to detail the information he had received from two of his intelligence officers— Capt. John Brown and Ensign Henry DeBerniere. The two men had been ordered to gather information west of Boston. They spent a week mixing with the locals in the towns around Lexington and Concord, Massachusetts, and had reported that there was a major munitions depot concealed in Concord, and that both Hancock and Adams were basing themselves in Lexington.

"Here, gentlemen, is an opportunity!" On the final word, the general smacked the desktop hard with the flat of his hand.

"We put the king's orders in motion with a raid on the Concord depot. We then augment the captured munitions with two patriot leaders to boot!"

Fixing his eyes on Smith alone, the general slowed his words and lowered his tone: "And Colonel, I trust I do not need to add that I will not have a debacle of the sort we encountered at the supply depot at Salem, Massachusetts, in February of this year."

Colonel Smith averted his eyes, staring with mock concentration at the papers on the table before him.

A debacle indeed, thought Pitcairn. A debacle of the very worst sort—an embarrassment to the crown. On February 27, a British command, 240 men strong under Col. Alexander Leslie, had been stopped just yards short of its target, a munitions storage depot in Salem. The locals had ripped up the planks on the South River Bridge, then proceeded to haul the munitions, including cannon, out of reach, as Leslie's men stood and watched. On their return trip to Boston, the British soldiers had been jeered by the citizens of every town and village they traveled through.

The colonists obviously had known in advance of the British plans, no doubt a result of the loose lips of the king's soldiers, who had a propensity for discussing army business in Boston taverns and streets. It had been the same with the raid on Fort William and Mary: Paul Revere had freely ridden to Portsmouth and warned his countrymen. Even before the troops had been sent to reinforce the fort, the colonists had looted it on December 14—then returned for more the next day.

Major Pitcairn shuddered at the memory of the Salem fiasco, and at the unthinkable humiliation Colonel Leslie now endured: to be known forever as Leslie the Timid by all who spoke his name. He wondered if this was what Colonel Smith was thinking now. He thanked God the general had not directed his warning at him.

"No, Colonel Smith, you will succeed." General Gage handed Smith the campaign order. "I have prepared this personally, to eliminate the possibility of the information being passed on to the colonials."

While Smith looked over the brief order, the general continued: "I have developed this plan of action without consulting anyone other than the navy. Surprise is of absolute importance.

"You, with the support of Major Pitcarin"—and here Gage turned his gaze directly at the major, who tried to change his grimace into something like a smile—"will place your best grenadier and light-infantry companies on off duty until I send you the order to march. The men will be provisioned for two days. As we speak, longboats are being anchored in the harbor, to be ready at a few hours' notice to move your troops across to the Cambridge shore."

Colonel Smith, head nodding, wattles bobbing, was doing his best to read his orders and listen to the commander at the same time. When the general finished, he lifted his head from the paper to speak.

"General," he said, "if we burn one or two of their towns, would that not send a strong message?"

"Only that we are savages, Colonel," Gage replied icily. Pitcarin winced. Smith's idiocy was just the sort that could derail his own career, if only through the following of his orders.

"Arrest the leaders and eliminate their munitions," Gage continued. "Take no steps beyond that. To destroy homes and villages would only inflame the populace. We are undermanned, Colonel, have you forgotten? We can barely hold New England without having to contend with the southern colonies as well."

Colonel Smith looked sheepish. "Yes, sir," he said softly. "When do we attack?"

"You, the navy, and Major Mitchell will have six hours' notice. Mitchell will command a force of forty men and officers; they will cross Boston Neck and spread out along the highways west and north with instructions to intercept all colonial messengers. Mitchell knows nothing of our plans, nor will he. The same is true of the navy. We will not be thwarted this time by the leakage of information."

"Sir . . ." Smith began. He appeared in pain. Pitcarin closed his eyes, waiting for what would come next.

General Gage spoke: "Colonel Smith, you have your written orders. What is it that you do not understand? You are both dismissed."

10

APRIL 18, 1775
FITCH'S TAVERN,
BEDFORD, MASSACHUSETTS

IT HAD BEEN A LONG DAY. The ride from Boston to Bedford took until early evening; it was past seven when he arrived at his brother-in-law's house, his clothes wet from a spring rain and his oxen bedraggled and in sore need of food. He wanted only to bake and dry in front of the fireplace, feel the warmth return to his bones, eat a simple meal, and sleep until morning. Tomorrow would be another full day—eight hours, at least, to Amherst, then more work to do there.

Jonathan must have heard the wagon creaking into the barnyard; he was out the back door before Thompson Maxwell had even climbed down.

"Thompson, you've arrived at the perfect time. I didn't know when you'd be here. I was on my way to Fitch's Tavern to meet with the Committee of Safety. Join me, won't you? We're meeting to discuss the latest from the Lexington committee, news of great concern."

Jonathan began helping Thompson unhitch the oxen and cover the goods, dismissing his protestations all the while. As they worked, he brought his brother-in-law abreast of the latest news: "Since you were last here, we have received town funding to pay for twenty-five minutemen—one shilling a week for each. The best of the Bedford

militia have volunteered. All around Boston, Thompson, it is happening like this—towns are choosing their best and most loyal from
the militia. Minutemen—to be ready at a minute's notice. It's happening everywhere. And just in time, too, I believe. But come; we
will be late for the meeting. There will be a nice fire at the tavern."

Thompson stopped his protests. As tired as he was, he was beginning to warm to thoughts of an evening at Fitch's Tavern, where the
talk would be of liberty and revolution, not of farming, planting, and
the dull daily affairs of the courthouse, as it so often was in Jones
Tavern at home.

Amherst seemed almost another world to him now: peaceful,
complacent, isolated from the mounting tensions that seethed to the
south and east. Tories in Amherst, men such as Joshua Atherton,
were still preaching negotiation and compromise with King George.
But not here. Not in Bedford, Massachusetts, which seemed nearly as
fervid, almost as much a hotbed of revolution as was Boston itself.

Thirty minutes later, they were at the door to the tavern, being
greeted by the proprietor, Jeremiah Fitch, who was passing with a
tray of rum-filled mugs. The balding, round-faced taverner was
dressed in his usual stained apron, spotted with soot and samples of
the evening meal.

"Welcome, Jonathan. And you, Mr. Maxwell, it's good to see you
again. I trust that things are well with you and your family in New
Hampshire?"

This was just the sort of moment that Thompson Maxwell loved.
Only in a village tavern, he thought to himself, and perhaps only in
New England: hearty, robust proprietors presiding over smoky, boisterous rooms; palpable camaraderie; the spirits and the fellowship
flowing equally all night. Along with the politics—most of it Whig—
and the small, often valuable nuggets of gossip that passed among
drinkers as freely as the rum.

"I have moved a group of tables to the corner for you," said
Fitch. "Most of your company are already there."

As they approached the table, Thompson saw that he knew many of the men seated there. Some he had known since his childhood in Bedford; others he had met in his frequent comings and goings from Bedford in the past several years.

Even so, Jonathan introduced every man as proudly as he would a brother "First Lt. Moses Abbott, Second Lt. Timothy Jones, Sgt. Christopher Page, Sgt. Asa Fassett, Sgt. Seth Saultmarsh, Sgt. Ebenezer Fitch."

He finished, and Thompson and the men exchanged greetings. That done, Jonathan raised his voice to make an announcement: "I would like to start tonight by having Timothy read what a man named Patrick Henry said recently in the Virginia House of Burgesses. I hadn't known those southerners possessed such passion for the cause of liberty. Go ahead, Timothy."

With that, Lieutenant Jones leaned closer to the lantern, bent his head, and began reading:

"There is no retreat but in submission and slavery! Our chains are forged. Their clanking may be heard on the plains of Boston! The war is inevitable—and let it come!

"It is in vain, sir, to extenuate the matter. Gentleman may cry, 'Peace! Peace!'—but there is no peace. The war has actually begun! The next gale that sweeps down from the north will bring to our ears the clash of resounding arms! Our brethren are already in the field! Why stand we here idle? What is it that gentlemen wish? What would they have? Is life so dear, or peace so sweet, as to be purchased at the price of chains and slavery? Forbid it, Almighty God! I know not what course others may take, but as for me, give me liberty or give me death!"

It was quiet for a moment while Jones leaned back in his chair. "By God," said one of the men, "that Henry fellow could be from Massachusetts!" There was general laughter and cheering from one end of the table to the other.

"Yes," Jonathan added, "he has the same passion for freedom."

"And the same fire as Mr. Adams," another man put in, "but Adams would have taken an hour to say the same thing."

This sent the group into gales of laughter. When they subsided, the talk turned to Adams and Hancock, then to the state of affairs in Boston and in the colonies to the south. This brought Thompson to relate what he had seen and heard in the city earlier that day—longboats being lowered from the British ships in the harbor rowed up the Charles River, then hauled up on the Boston shore across from the Cambridge marsh.

"There is no doubt something is about to happen. Paul Revere received word from a stable boy who works at Gage's Province House that the regulars are about to march. Revere is said to think the longboats mean they will row over to Cambridge rather than across Boston Neck. He isn't certain, though."

The talk went on for another hour, of British tactics, the safety of munitions, the timetable for revolution, the state of mind of Parliament and the king. Long before it ended, Thompson Maxwell had nodded off.

Earlier that same day, in Boston, Colonel Smith had called a meeting of the officers of the light-infantry companies chosen for the Concord raid. His manner was the traditional British military one: steely, autocratic, devoid of feeling. Major Pitcarin, watching from the edge of the circle of officers, wondered yet again how it was the king's army could be as successful as it was with so many of Smith's type—aristocrats who purchased their commands—as high as they were in its chain of command.

"Two days ago," the colonel told his men, "you were put on notice that a raid was planned to deprive the provincial militia of its munitions and supplies. You were not informed of the time or the specific target. The time is tonight."

He paused dramatically, sweeping the room with his look. "Immediately after dark, each of you will order your sergeants to quietly awaken their men and have them assemble on the drill ground.

Stealth, stealth is the word of the day." He waved his hands vaguely in the air for effect.

"We must not alert Boston to our leaving," he went on. "Until the moment we assemble, you will tell no one other than your sergeants of the plan."

As Smith described the orders of the day, his voice rose to the level of a bullhorn. Pitcarin shook his head sadly. Even through closed windows, he thought, the timetable for the raid could be heard half a block away.

"And on the way to the Concord arsenal, we're going to capture those bastard troublemakers, Sam Adams and John Hancock," the colonel declared. "General Gage has received orders from King George to ship the ringleaders to London to be hanged."

He heaved a satisfied sigh, wiped his brow, and let his hands fall to his sides. A moment passed and the assembly remained still, in some facsimile of respect. He looked from his men to Pitcarin and back again, and his face began to redden as he realized what he had forgotten: "You have your orders, now go! You are dismissed!"

When they had reached what they must have thought was a permissible distance, the officers broke into an excited hum, then filed out of the building amid raucous predictions of colonial bungling and the "surprise" in store for the "turkey hunters" and their friends.

Colonel Smith's orders were carried out to the letter. On the way to enacting his part in them, however, one young officer stopped to purchase tobacco and was drawn into conversation with the shopkeeper's attractive daughter. Within minutes of his departure, a messenger was on his way to Paul Revere's home.

Two sergeants made their own quick stop, for some rum to chase away the growing chill as the day drew toward a close. There was hardly a tavern keeper in Boston who was not a patriot, and this one was no exception. Again, within minutes, the news was on its way to Paul Revere.

Earlier in the day, one William Dawes had been among the last travelers passing through the fortifications at Boston Neck. He could not help but notice that the security had been increased, and that the gates at the guard station were being closed to civilians; it seemed he had come through just in time. Dawes, like the taverner and the shopkeeper's daughter, felt it his duty to carry the news that the land exit from the city was now sealed.

Boston was a small town. Little escaped notice, least of all the eight hundred men, each loaded down with musket, bayonet, cartridge box, and haversack, being marched through the streets and over the common by night, to the longboats moored by the shore.

The Sons of Liberty network had stationed watchers on the streets, in parks, and at windows: men and women, young boys and girls. Two young men were at a second-floor window on Beacon Hill overlooking an intersection. Before the British were even in sight, one turned to the other and exclaimed: "There they go now, the pride of the British army. I can tell from their heavy tread and the rattling of their arms." And indeed it was the grenadiers, with their towering caps of bearskin and white metal faceplates; and the light infantry in tight caps of leather. And within minutes, this too was known by Paul Revere.

The patriots were prepared. By ten o'clock, two lanterns were lit in the belfry of the old North Church, indicating that the British were coming by boat, across the Charles River to Cambridge. Revere himself was rowed across the Charles by two friends—to be ready to warn Adams and Hancock in Lexington, and the militia in Concord, of the regulars' approach. Dawes and other couriers left also, fanning out to towns off his path, so that he might reach Lexington and Concord before the British came ashore.

As Paul Revere reached Cambridge and secured the horse held ready for him, the last of the British were crossing the Charles. In the last longboat, Major Pitcarin sat disconsolately as Colonel Smith expressed the sentiment that had been overheard in a thousand Boston taverns and shops: "One volley from our regulars and we'll put them to flight like rabbits. A few towns burned would set everything right."

The landing location Smith had chosen was the Cambridge marsh—making it necessary to disembark and wade through water and mud 150 yards to reach solid ground. It was now two in the morning. The men had assembled and were ready to march.

In columns, they sloshed in wet and muddy boots and trousers, no longer the polished army that had left Boston only ninety minutes earlier. The night was cold; the men were wet and freezing. A bedraggled formation made its way to Lexington.

Almost before they had reached the center of Cambridge, Colonel Smith knew all hope of surprise had been lost. Men and women were peering out of windows, screaming insults as the column of soldiers marched past. The sounds of guns and church bells could be heard in the distance as they passed through Arlington.

"Damn!" said Smith, as he turned to face Pitcarin. "Just like the Salem raid. And with only six hours' notice—how could they have known?"

It was decided, finally, to order messengers back to Boston, advising General Gage of the status of things and requesting that reinforcements be sent. Officers and sergeants went from company to company, trying futilely to muffle the rising drone of protests from the cold, wet, and now disheartened men.

Major Pitcarin, watching idly from a distance as his commanding officer railed at yet another captive set of ears, was struck suddenly by an unbidden mental image: his career, like his uniform, wet and in tatters, splotched by mud and, soon perhaps, unless he was lucky, torn by musket fire.

The image froze into his mind as he led his small band of men squishing and sloshing their way down the Lexington Road.

11

IT WAS A CHILLY LATE-SPRING NIGHT IN BEDFORD. Thompson Maxwell lay under wool blankets in a first-floor room in his brother-in-law's house, dreaming of his days as a ranger in the French War, and of the first man who'd died at his hands—an Indian, near Lake George in the Adirondacks—in the spring of his seventeenth year.

He woke with a start. Something loud, and very heavy, had struck the house and seemed to cause it to shake. His heart thudded. He jumped from his bed and cast about for his trousers on the floor.

"What in blazes was that?" he cried out at the darkness.

There were shouts from just outside the house, not far from his bedroom window: "Captain Wilson, Captain Wilson! The British are coming! British regulars are coming this way!"

The outline of his brother-in-law appeared briefly in the doorway. "It's all right, Thompson. It's just the signal we agreed upon."

"What, a boulder hurled at the side of the house?" Thompson muttered, but Jonathan had already passed by. Thompson heard him open a window at the end of the hall and call back to the messenger. Seconds later he was back, standing in his underwear in the doorway of Thompson's room: "You were right," Jonathan told him. "A large force of British regulars is on its way from Cambridge along the Lexington Road. General Gage must be out to raid the Concord supplies. I have passed the word—the entire Bedford company is assembling at Fitch's Tavern at dawn."

Thompson had pulled on his shirt and trousers.

"Jonathan, Hancock is in Lexington, in the path of the British. We must warn him—they will surely want to capture him."

"No need. Our call came from Lexington. He must have been warned by now, and is safe. Thompson, if you are willing, my company and I would welcome your help. Will you come?"

Thompson nodded as he gathered his pack and provisions. "You needn't have asked," he said.

"Good. If you will get the horses ready, then. I would like to spend a few moments to ease the fears of the family."

It was a bright, clear, cold night, perhaps an hour before dawn. Thompson waited with the horses near the front of the house. He could see the faces of Jonathan's family at the windows—his own sister and Jonathan's two children. Before three minutes had passed, his brother-in-law arrived beside him, musket in hand. The two men mounted their horses. In the distance, the peals of church bells broke the silence of the night.

Arriving at Fitch's Tavern minutes later, they were met by a dozen Bedford minutemen. The entire Fitch family was up and bustling about. Young Lydia Fitch had stoked the fire to warm the morning, and was beginning a breakfast of hot buttered rum and cold cornmeal mush. The smells caused Thompson to think briefly of his wife, Sybel: asleep, oblivious, some forty miles farther north.

By dawn all the members of the Bedford Minuteman Company, as well as a large number of volunteer militia, had gathered at the tavern. The mood was almost festive—the room echoed with loud voices, laughter, and jokes. Thompson, of course, had seen this before and knew it for what it was: the nervous bravado of fearful men facing danger and an uncertain fate.

"They'll know soon they should have stayed in Boston!" one voice shouted over the din.

"Better yet, back in England," called out another.

"They'll have two coats of red before the day is done—one wool, the other blood! Liberty! This is the beginning!"

Thompson, Jonathan, and man named John Moore, a militia captain, adjourned to the inn's sitting room to confer. Without argument, it was agreed: Their destination should be Concord—the objective of the British—rather than Lexington, which the redcoats, no doubt, would have passed through already, by the time they reached that town.

Back in the main tavern room, Captain Wilson called for quiet, then addressed the assembled men: "It's a cold breakfast, boys, but we'll give the British a hot dinner. We'll have every dog of them before nightfall. Outside! We march to Concord, now!"

The sergeants ordered the men into columns of twos. No two of them wore the same clothes or carried the same muskets or packs. Their mood, still boisterous, still jaunty, contrasted starkly with the small, bleak-faced groups of family members huddled along the road against the early-morning chill, watching silently as their men marched stoically by. A few children held to their mothers' skirts, some weeping quietly. Young wives searched out the faces of their husbands among the marchers, each one wondering if it would prove her last glimpse.

Thompson was struck by the sadness and fear in their eyes, and, though only briefly, by a pang of melancholy that none of those eyes watched for him. For the second time that morning, his thoughts turned to Sybel, and to Jonathan, who must be holding fast to images of his own wife, Thompson's sister. There are heartaches here aplenty, Thompson thought.

Sounds of church bells and musket fire grew louder. The alarm had been widely sounded, Thompson knew, and with it, he realized that the Bedford militia was anything but alone.

As if to echo his thoughts, as they came around a turn in the road, three more militia companies—minutemen from Carlisle, Acton, and Chelmsford—called out their greetings and fell in alongside.

A half mile from the North Bridge in Concord, they came around yet another turn and witnessed a sight that had to quicken the heartbeat of every marcher in the line: five hundred armed men at least, by Thompson's estimate, assembled, four and five deep, on the south hill overlooking the bridge. Most, like the Bedford militia, were tattered and motley, in clothes that ranged from workday to Sunday best, with the single exception of one town's militia, who appeared at least to have tried: Their jackets, and hats when they wore them, were all in a range of blue hues.

Thompson, Jonathan, and Captain Moore hurried ahead to determine who was in charge. As they neared the band of colonials, the North Bridge came into full view and Thompson got his first sight of the enemy: a thin wall of red jackets, the British Light Infantry, just thick enough to block any view of the landscape behind them, on either side of the bridge.

On reaching the hillside, they were directed to a Colonel Barrett. A miller by trade, Barrett was the commander of the Concord, Massachusetts, militia, and had taken charge of the arriving troops. It was Jonathan who took it upon himself to make the introductions: "Colonel Barrett, I am Capt. Jonathan Wilson, commander of the Bedford Minuteman Company. This is Captain Moore of the Bedford militia, and Thompson Maxwell, a lieutenant in the Amherst, New Hampshire, militia."

Barrett greeted them curtly. Jonathan went on to describe his company, then asked how the men should be deployed.

"I would appreciate it, Captain, if your men could be placed on the west hillside, behind the stone wall."

Barrett gestured to his left, indicating the location he had in mind. Jonathan listened, then spoke briefly, alone, with Captain

Moore, who then departed to put the company in position. As Moore turned to go, Jonathan faced Colonel Barrett: "Lieutenant Maxwell was one of Rogers's Rangers in the French War," he said. "We are lucky to have him with us on an occasion such as this."

Barrett's only response was the searching look he gave Thompson—after which he turned to face Jonathan again: "I hope we will soon have more support from New Hampshire than just you, Lieutenant."

As Thompson and other officers huddled with Colonel Barrett, other militia commanders were coming into view: Bedford, Carlisle, Chelmsford, Groton, Acton, Westford, Lincoln. They were gaining strength by the minute. And the British at the bridge were not many—it would not be long, thought Thompson, before the numbers boded well.

"Why are the militia units here and not in Concord center, where the British are?" It was a newly arrived commander from Acton, a man not older than twenty-five.

Colonel Barrett made no answer right away. Instead, he motioned with both hands for the officers—there were perhaps two dozen now—to gather close around him. When the circle had narrowed to his satisfaction, he began to talk:

"We were in Concord center waiting for them when they arrived from Lexington. We had received the news already—at least eight Lexington minutemen killed, ten more gravely wounded, the British on the common, bayoneting those too injured to flee. The minutemen could do nothing; they were outnumbered ten to one.

"And so we chose not to have a repeat of that in Concord, and withdrew across the North Bridge. There is no purpose to foolish bravery. Better to wait for more reinforcements. As you can see, they are arriving as we speak."

"Surely things have evened up by now," one of the officers said.

Barrett straightened to his full height, in no mood to have his command decisions questioned at this early stage.

"I ordered our units to withdraw to this position. In view of the rout at Lexington, I believed caution was in order. I continue to believe so. The numbers are improving. We now have four hundred men, and more are coming by the minute."

He gestured toward the British units on either side of the bridge. "They can see the same things we can—the fresh troops arriving. I think they know they'll be badly outnumbered before long."

Thompson looked around and saw that it was true. More patriot militia companies were pouring in from every side; the British were hemmed in on a narrow road; they could bring only a few guns to bear. The colonists, by contrast, were spread out on the hillside in a wide arc, though only a few of the militia units were close enough to be effective.

"Colonel, might I suggest that we move our units closer to the bridge, to be in closer range?" It was the officer from Acton again.

Barrett was silent for some moments. Thompson felt sure he knew what the man was thinking: Proximity worked both ways. The sight of a single dead minuteman could send a collection of troops such as this one—untrained, ill equipped, unused to the sights and sounds of death—scattering for the hills. Reluctantly, Barrett ordered the Concord and Acton units fifty yards closer to the bridge, while other units were sent to take protected positions behind the stone wall overlooking it, roughly twenty-five yards closer than they were.

The officers ran to rejoin their units, which moved forward slowly to their new positions. Reinforcements continued to arrive. The sight of them—and their own relative safety in the hillsides around the bridge—served to embolden the men:

"Murderers!" "Butchers!" "See how brave you are now!" they cried.

The minutes passed. The colonists' numbers continued to swell. The shouts and jeers slowly died. Soon, the quiet was unnerving— the calm before a certain storm

Suddenly, from his position in the rear, Thompson saw that the column of militiamen was beginning to advance, behind the beat of drummer boy Abner Hosmer.

"They're moving back!" came a call from men on the road and on the hillside.

The sight of the retreating British caused the colonists to quicken their pace. A widening arc of militia, two and three deep, was moving steadily down the hill, along the road and riverbank toward the bridge and its knot of British troops. The two companies of light infantry that had not yet moved from the north side of the bridge now seemed to panic: The men rushed back over the bridge in a pell-mell fashion, colliding with those on the south side. Pressed together as they were on the narrow road, they would be all but helpless if the militia continued its pace.

Then from somewhere near the rear came a single agonized cry: "They're burning Concord!"

Thompson looked to the south. It was true. Clouds of black, billowing smoke, from the general direction of Concord center, curled through the clear April sky.

The men, especially those of the Concord militia, became instantly enraged. They surged at the bridge far more quickly than Colonel Barrett had planned. The faces of the British regulars clustered on the road to the south of the bridge betrayed their panic; the redcoat commanders called for order, to no avail.

A shot rang out, then two more. Capt. Isaac Davis of Acton was struck in the heart, fell where he stood, and died instantly. The blood spurting from his wound sprayed the faces and boots of those closest by, some of whom, too stunned to do otherwise, stooped and pulled his inert body from the ground.

Another volley rang out from the south of the bridge, and young drummer Abner Hosmer was thrown back against the legs of the man behind him by the impact of a musket ball in the head. The militia's forward movement stalled, then stopped.

Thompson saw the halt. He knew that command must be taken

instantly, or the panic would become general and all would be lost. He dropped to one knee and raised his musket reflexively, wondering how long he should wait for the order to come. Just then, it did—from Colonel Barrett and Major Buttrick of Concord, almost as one: "Fire, fire! For God's sake, fire!"

Captain Wilson was only seconds behind them with the command for the Bedford minutemen: "Aim for the officers! The reddest coats! Fire!"

Within seconds, the crackle and dull bark of hundreds of muskets were everywhere. The smell of powder was overpowering, the smoke so thick that the bridge was no longer visible to units in the rear. Faces and throats were burning from the powder flash. But even the greenest recruits were too exhilarated not to press on.

Thompson, pausing to reload, looked toward the bridge as a breeze briefly cleared the smoke. The British were retreating: running, stumbling into their fellow soldiers, tripping over their wounded and dead. More than a dozen bodies lay on the bridge and road as the light infantry fled back the way it had come.

Thompson turned and surveyed the colonials. Some—a few—were cheering. Most appeared stunned, staring at the bodies of the dead and wounded in silence, or gazing straight ahead, apparently at nothing, their muskets dangling, forgotten, from their hands.

He knew the shock of the first battle, the first sight of death—and even beyond the first, it was a shock—and felt for these men, even more for those among them who looked to be little more than boys.

Still not moving, startled by their success, the patriots watched, mostly mute, as a wounded British private hopped on one foot in an attempt to join his fleeing comrades, his blood forming a thin red trail in the dry road.

There would be no turning now, thought Colonel Barrett. In Lexington the dead had been colonists; now there were British dead and wounded on the ground. The enormity of it sobered him: He was a miller, yet with ultimate responsibility for the lives and deaths of men. And today, for perhaps the first and last time in his life, he had the power to change a piece of the world. "Cease fire! Cease fire!" he called out. Turning to his officers and sergeants, he gave his orders: "Tell your men to form into companies. Reload, then have the commanders of each company join me here."

On the north side of the bridge, the men from Acton were carrying off their two dead. The British casualties on the bridge and the road appeared to have been abandoned. The colonists had watched as two wounded officers were carried away on the shoulders of their men; now, two privates were attempting to drag themselves back along the road. Their colleagues, though still within sight, made no move to help.

"At least we care for our fallen," Jonathan muttered.

Six militia commanders by now were with Colonel Barrett, with others arriving singly and in twos. The colonel seemed impatient. He did not wish to wait.

"We have not won," he began. "Understand that, please. We have only begun to be tested."

The officers around him looked puzzled. A few shook their heads.

"We must stay together. We must stay resolved, or all that we gained will be lost. Already, some of our men are wandering home; they have seen that this was not a drill, they have seen their friends dying, they want no more of it. But more will come, I have no doubt.

"But if we fail to stay together, if we weaken or disperse, the British will return and destroy us. They will burn our towns, make a lesson of our humiliation for the other colonies to witness. It will be the end, and our only legacy will be disgrace."

He paused, then looked around at the men surrounding him.

"Your opinions? Please, I urge you, speak up."

Several voices spoke at once. A few proposed disbanding and returning home; others insisted on pursuing the British to the town center and reengaging them there. For the first several minutes, Jonathan was silent. Then, when it seemed clear there was to be no common accord, he opened his mouth to speak: "Sir, I know none of you or your military backgrounds, and I mean no disrespect. But Thompson Maxwell here was a member of Rogers's Rangers in the French War. Personally, I would like his opinion."

Thompson was not eager for leadership, but when asked, he was not one to withhold it. And his opinions, in this instance, were strong. He nodded quickly to Jonathan, then turned to face the colonel.

"Sir," he said, "I don't think they will return here. We have the secure high ground, and the river as a buffer. I think they will retreat to gather an increased force. They must see, as I do, a tidal wave of colonials converging. They are outnumbered; they cannot help but know it. I believe they will return to Boston."

A couple of local officers muttered unpleasantly, unhappy with such views. Thompson ignored them and continued.

"It would be wise, perhaps, to send a dozen or so of your Concord men across the bridge to gather information. If they report back that the situation is as I believe, then I would recommend sending the rest of the men across the bridge, to move east under the cover of woods and fields north of the Lexington Road. The British will be strung out, less ready for defense than when in their formations. Surprise attacks along the road would weaken them further before they can regroup or increase their numbers."

Barrett looked doubtful at this. Thompson sighed—he thought he knew why. But soft thoughts of the "honorable" way to fight, in the open with blocked formations, had no place in a battle such as this.

"Sir," he continued. "I mean no disrespect. But we simply must press any advantage we can. This is a well-trained, well-provisioned army we are fighting. We must fight them like Indians, not like British. Attack, withdraw east, attack again. Always from cover."

"Yes," agreed Jonathan. "We are no match for them on their terms. We could deplete them slowly this way, and keep them off balance. It is the only chance we have."

By now there were close to twenty-five officers in the group. One of them, an older man with gray hair and a handsome mustache, stepped forward. It was apparent that he knew Barrett well.

"James," he began, then stopped. "Colonel, sir. I also was in the French War, as you know. What this officer says is right, absolutely right."

For a full sixty seconds, Colonel Barrett said nothing, only stared hard at his right boot, which drew wide, precise circles in the dirt. Then he looked up.

"Send the scouts," he said. "But there will be no firing, no firing for any reason except as a last line of defense."

Again, it was Thompson's turn: "And stay clear of the light infantry. Their first duty is flanking. You don't want to be between them and the main British force."

He doubted seriously that any of the men understood the implication of what he had just said, even Jonathan, who possessed courage and determination along with moderate skills as a soldier. Jonathan could be incautious at times, even reckless when he felt he held the upper hand. It was a dangerous trait. Thompson, at that moment, resolved silently to stay close to his brother-in-law.

One by one, the officers left to return to their companies with the new orders. Within minutes, the first of the scouts could be seen heading down the road toward the bridge.

Not more than fifteen minutes later, from just beyond the bridge, came the cry: "They're retreating! They're going back down the Lexington Road!"

It set off a chain reaction. The men erupted, almost as one: "Get the bastards!" "No mercy for murderers!" "Kill the town-burners!"

A cluster of men closest to the bridge, twenty or thirty in all, swept across it at a full run. The others watched, paused briefly, some looking uncertainly at their officers, then went too. Within seconds, seven hundred men, a stream of shrieking, disordered humanity, were surging across the bridge almost as a body, then into the fields and woods toward the Lexington Road.

Most headed for the wooded Ripley and Arrowhead ridges, which overlooked the road. All order was lost. Some units remained together; most fragmented into small, random clusters, which then joined with others as the stream thinned and spread. No one was in charge. The officers, except for their uniforms, were indistinguishable from their men.

The first British they encountered were in a company of light infantry moving east, through thick woods, about three hundred feet off the road. On hearing the mass of men closing behind them, then catching sight of their leaders, the British fired a volley, but the distance was too great for the balls to find their marks. As they were reloading, groups of militia closed the distance, then stopped and fired from the cover of trees.

Three light infantry soldiers fell dead and three more were wounded, among them an officer. They ran south, in open panic now, as musket balls whizzed around them and struck the trees, rocks, and earth. Two more fell, one rolling in the dirt, screaming and clutching his thigh, the blood on his trousers mixed with the old, caked mud from the Charles River. Only the fallen officer was dragged back toward the main column, his arms around two men. Wounded regulars were left where they fell.

All along the Lexington Road, the militia streamed forward: firing from trees, hilltops, and stone walls, then taking cover as the British returned fire, then reloading, advancing, and firing again.

Now the half a dozen horse carts, appropriated by Colonel Smith in Concord for bearing supplies, were being used as crude tumbrils, to pick up fallen officers and return them to the rear. Rank-and-file soldiers continued to be left where they fell.

Thompson Maxwell, running through the woods at the tail end

of the long column of orderless, marauding militiamen, heard new firing from south of the Lexington Road. Fresh units from towns south of Lexington and Concord, he thought, to add to the imbalance—the ratio must be nearing ten to one. So numbers were no longer a worry. Today, at least, would go the colonists' way.

But from what he had seen in the last fifteen minutes, there were certain to be darker days ahead.

12

MAJOR PITCARIN WAS AT A LOSS. Never before in his twenty-year career had he experienced anything that compared to this. Panic, chaos, an enemy who disappeared behind trees and into woods, who picked off his men like ducks in a pond from unseen positions, then retreated too quickly for an accurate shot. There was nothing, nothing in his experience that prepared him for this. It was like doing battle against ghosts.

His men had not slept in more than thirty hours. They were tired and hungry, and utterly untrained for the type of battle they were facing. They had been drilled to fight as units, not as individuals, and in open areas, not against an enemy that came at them from behind rocks. Only in the French War had the major heard of anything like this—and that had been against savages, not men of English blood.

Pitcarin did not know what to tell his men, or how to lead them, how to keep control, even how to protect their lives. He felt, for the first time, that he was failing his command.

It was a few minutes after noon and still six miles to Lexington. There were not enough light infantry to shield the long column from attack, which was now coming from both sides of the road. Suddenly, as he watched, one of his officers, a man with nearly a decade of experience, bolted from the ranks and rushed over a stone wall and into the trees, a squad of grenadiers behind him, screaming as he went, "Stand up and face us! You're cowards, all of you!"

Pitcarin swore to himself, at the same time shouting at the man to come back. But it was too late. The officer spun around and slumped to the ground, struck in the shoulder by a musket ball. The rest of the squad, after witnessing the loss of their commander, retreated quickly to the safety of their ranks. A pair of privates grabbed the officer beneath the arms and dragged him back to his unit, leaving behind one of the regulars draped lifeless over a stone wall.

Pitcarin, jaw set, watched the man being helped. From a few feet away, where a handful of grenadiers were watching also, he heard one of them mutter, not thinking he could be heard: "Let the light infantry rummage in the woods; it's what they're trained to do."

The major almost laughed. All these men would be learning new skills before this war was done, he thought. The colonists had learned from their battles with the Indians; the British would have done well to follow suit. Their only innovation since the French War was the creation of light infantry to flank and protect the main column—and now even these men were too exhausted and depleted to do any good. Not that he would be able to convince Colonel Smith of that. Still, he would have to try. The soldiers would continue to be easy targets for these farmers with their turkey muskets if the rules were not changed soon.

A captain on horseback pulled up in front of him, hysterical and out of breath:

"Major, Major, sir! I'm losing control of my men! They have heard the rumor that the colonials are scalping our wounded, and are about to desert ranks!"

"That's a damn lie!" Pitcarin screamed into the officer's face. Then he caught himself, lowering his voice instantly—any display of panic from him would be the surest route to chaos in the ranks.

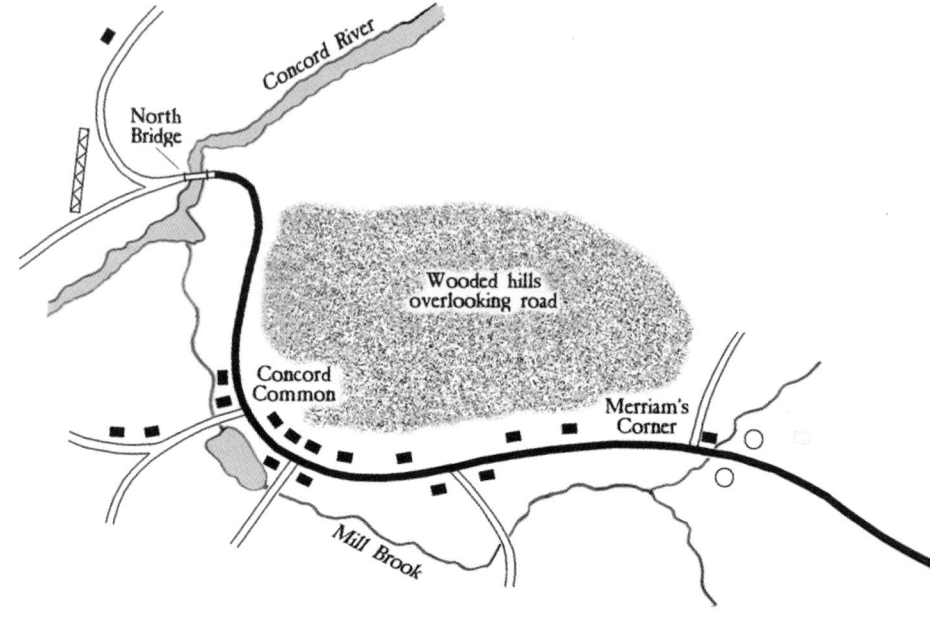

"Calm yourself, Captain. I know the origin of that rumor, and that's all it is. Lieutenant Leslie, who commanded the company at the North Bridge, told of one rebel who struck a wounded man with an ax, but the incident was isolated—it was not repeated.

"Captain, understand this: The colonials are angry. We are fighting an army of very angry men. They saw us bayonet their wounded on Lexington Common; then we burned their militia supplies in Concord, which, I am told by Lieutenant Leslie, they thought was the village itself.

"But gain control, Captain. Your enemy is angry, not invincible. Perhaps it might help if you found a touch of anger yourself." He waved his arm in the general direction of the officer's command. "Now get back there and get control of your men!"

The captain seemed about to speak, but then pitched forward, uttered a single low grunt, and slumped against the major. Grabbing him to stop his fall, Pitcarin saw the fountain of blood pumping from

Map of British Retreat from Concord on April 18, 1775
Thompson Maxwell's fight in Concord from the North Bridge to
Bloody Curve.

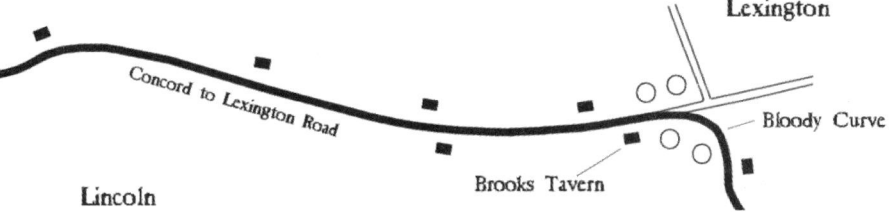

Fight at Concord
April 19, 1775

▬ Route of British Retreat
○ Major Skirmishes
■ Houses and Structures
〰〰〰 American Militia Assembly Area

the wound in his side. Turning to two grenadiers on their way past
on horseback, he gave an abrupt order, which he hoped managed to
conceal the mounting panic he felt: "You two! Carry this officer to
the cart up ahead. Then inform his unit that he has fallen—wounded—that he will no longer be discharging his duties this day!"

Major Pitcarin knew: The shot was meant for him. He had been
on horseback, an easy target, but the shooter had fired low, and the
captain had stepped in the way. Pitcarin had been spared. For how
much longer, or for what fate, he could not begin to know.

"Six more miles through hell," he muttered to himself.

Jonathan and Thompson, with two Concord militia commanders, ran east through the woods to set an ambush site ahead of the

British column. The crossroads, Merriam's Corner, was the chosen spot. It was the last area in Concord where heavy woods overlooked the road.

Thompson guessed that six hundred colonial soldiers were now moving east toward the site. In the woods overlooking the crossroads they were met by four new militia companies: from Chelmsford, Reading, Billerica, and Tewksbury. Their number must now be over a thousand, with more to come. And still no sign of the British.

It was a perfect site. The main road at Merriam's Corner crossed a bridge over a north–south stream; even better, the stream cut through a ravine in the wooded hill on the north side of the road. The British light infantry, moving east parallel to the road to Lexington, would have to return to the road at Merriam's Corner to cross the stream, then climb back up the wooded slope to protect the flanks of Colonel Smith's force.

The companies by now were arriving in force. Having regained loose control, Colonel Barrett, with two newly arrived officers, ordered their units onto the wooded slope east of the stream. A Colonel Green, from Billerica, gave the orders: "Remain behind rocks and trees. Stay as far back from the road as you can and still have a good shot."

The order was taken up by company commanders farther down the Lexington Road. As new companies showed up, they took their place on the hillside. Less than an hour after the earliest arrivals, the last company was in place.

A calm settled over the crossroads. Except for the occasional barking of distant musket shots, the only proximate sound was the breaking of a twig, or a rock dislodged by a boot. All was quiet.

The British column could be heard before it was seen. Approaching the crossroads and the bridge, marching heavily, the flank guard, as predicted, came down the hill west of the stream, then joined the road to cross the bridge.

Jonathan, sitting next to Thompson on the hillside, watching from their concealment as the British column neared, could not resist a whisper: "They are not so arrogant now, the peacocks."

Thompson nodded thoughtfully. It was true. No fife-and-drum accompaniment, only the scuffling tread of tired men and creaking ambulance carts.

"We'll give them their due here," said Jonathan with unconcealed relish.

The regulars were well past the bridge when Colonel Smith saw the colonists on the hillside. At first, he did not at seem concerned, perhaps assuming a small, independent band of snipers. Turning to his second-in-command, Major Pitcarin, he spoke briefly, in low tones. A moment later, though, his voice rang out clearly, and Thompson knew he intended to be heard: "Clear out those farmers!"

The words were barely out of his mouth when shots from the woods rent the air, though only a dozen or so. Pitcarin could be seen to hesitate. He looked back at his colonel, who shook his head and motioned him to continue on with the flankers to remove the threat. The column of British began to move at a brisker pace. Thompson, watching, could only shake his head: The colonel was heedless of the plight of those not on horseback—the sleepless, exhausted, in some cases wounded troops now marching dully toward the musket barrels waiting on the hillside.

Jonathan's command was the first: "Fire!" The others followed within seconds, from every point on the hillside, "Fire!" "Fire!" "Fire!" "Fire!" "Fire!"

The sound was deafening. The musket balls were thick as hail in the air. More than a dozen soldiers in the front column fell instantly, in the first volley; others dove to the dirt, or sought the protection of rocks and trees. Some, a few, returned fire, but to little effect. The colonists were too well protected: behind tree trunks and obscured by the billowing smoke.

The militia reloaded and fired again, with devastating results. The grenadiers, loaded down under heavy equipment, were ordered to attack the hillside, but as they slipped and slid their way up the slope, the colonists picked them off like rabbits in a box. Below them, on the road, most of the men in Colonel Smith's command were too panicked even to try to reload, All they wanted was to scramble for the open fields.

"Fire at the officers!" Thompson heard Jonathan order as the grenadiers came into view. Through the cloud of smoke, the two men saw many more go down. "Fall back and reload," cried Jonathan, as a handful of grenadiers reached the top of the slope. "Fire at them again. Kill the officers!"

The carnage was general, the dead and wounded were everywhere. The grenadiers, having given up even the thought of attacking the hill, had returned to the road. The colonists moved forward, sometimes virtually unopposed.

One company, under the command of a Captain Trull of Reading, under his orders had positioned themselves behind farm buildings and stone walls at close quarters to the road. The British light infantry, continuing its flanking orders, came up behind the Reading men, who—caught unprepared—were butchered in place, by bayonet and by sword.

Between the smoke on the hillside Thompson saw British soldiers dropping their muskets to lighten their loads. They could not be blamed; volley after volley of musket fire blanketed the area. And while most shots were from too far away to be effective, the noise and chaos alone were more than enough to strike fear.

It was not only the British who panicked. Here and there across the hillside could be seen small clusters of retreating colonial troops, looking dazed by the endlessness of the gun smoke and musket fire, fading back into the woods under cover of smoke and confusion. There were not enough of them, though, to turn the tide of the battle; and fresh militia, amazingly, continued to arrive.

As the last of the British column moved out of sight, Thompson looked over the scene. The dead and wounded, both men and horses, littered the road to the east of the bridge. Some men moaned, wept, or cried for help. Others lay still, in the center of pools of blood that seeped into the dry earth around them. Still others simply sat, waiting for the colonists to do with them what they would.

Thompson turned to Jonathan. "Take your men east. I'll meet you later. I want to go down to the road and have a word with some of the British wounded."

Jonathan issued the command immediately. "Bedford men, fall back and toward Lexington!" His spirits were at battle pitch. He was almost out of sight through the woods before Thompson thought to call after him: "Don't take any unnecessary risks! Stay well back from the road! "

He sighed. It was doubtful his brother-in-law could hear him, and less likely still that he would be heeded.

Thompson heard a lone musket shot; turning, he saw that someone had put a wounded horse out of its agony. He moved along down the road, coming across the discarded pack of a grenadier, then of a light-infantry private. Both had fewer than ten balls left. He looked up as a minuteman approached him.

"They prepared poorly," he said, rising to greet the man, whom he found to be Joshua Simonds of Lexington. The two men began to exchange views on the battle, then suddenly stopped, their attention arrested by the sound of a small voice to their rear: "Please help me, sir!"

Turning, they saw a child lying behind them just off the road, a boy of no more than eleven or twelve. Protruding from his red coat, which was tightly buttoned, was a fife.

As Simonds began to unbutton the coat, the boy spoke again, "Please don't kill me!" A rush of blood gurgled up from between a pair of buttons on his chest.

Simonds reached down and picked up the boy as gently as he could.

"Don't worry," he said. " I'll help you. I have a good friend nearby."

He turned without a word to Thompson, and carried the small body down the road. Silently, Thompson watched the pair recede until they were out of sight, then made his way, head lowered, toward the sounds of musket. Something about the day, he knew, had just changed. And one more vision of a bloodied, twelve-year-old British fifer begging for his life—would now join the others that nightly inhabited his dreams.

As the routed British column passed through Merriam's Corner on its way to Lexington, Major Pitcarin heard a horse's hooves close behind him. Turning, he saw Colonel Smith riding hard toward him, swearing loudly and smacking regulars with the side of his sword as he pushed through a light infantry company.

"Move! Move, damn you! Let me through!" Wounded men, barely able to stand, were knocked to the ground or pushed aside by Smith's boot.

"Dammit, Pitcarin, get your bloody flankers out! Clean out the rabble along the road! Get to it! Now!"

The encounter at Merriam's Corner had been a disaster—more than thirty men and officers lost, with twice that number wounded. The men were low on powder, shot, and strength; most of what kept them going, the major thought, was the sight of open land in the distance—less cover from which to be attacked again.

That, and rage. Pure, blind rage, the sort of mindless fury Pitcarin had witnessed only minutes before, as he watched a private repeatedly bayonet a wounded colonial until his life was gone, and even then plant his boot against the dead man's chest, extract, and plunge home again.

Fear and rage, thought the major—poor motivators indeed, yet they were just about all that was left.

Looking ahead, he saw the land open on either side of the road: farmers' fields, orchards, meadows, pastures. He felt some of his own tension lift. There were still woods, to be sure, but they were sparser now, and farther back from the road. Flanking would be easier; there were fewer places for the rebels to hide.

He could see a company of them in the distance, moving through the thin woods parallel to the road. They didn't seem to be making progress any faster than his own column—which would not allow time to set an ambush. He began to feel as if the worst might be over, that they might reach Lexington with the present numbers intact.

He spurred his horse to quicken its pace, intending to catch up with Colonel Smith before the column came to a turn in the road near a couple of farms and what looked to be a tavern. Just then, from a small hill to the south he heard the sound of muskets—probably too far away to be effective, he thought. Then the sounds of a commotion behind him. He turned in his saddle and looked in the direction of his troops.

The main column was losing its form before his eyes. The grenadiers, apparently in panic, were pushing forward, trampling their own wounded and causing a dangerous clotting in the middle of the group.

Ensign DeBerniere rode up beside him: "Sir, there's a large group of them moving up toward the road near the curve, just by those farmhouses ahead."

"Get the flankers around them. We'll have them trapped between the column and the woods."

No sooner was the order given than Pitcarin heard a new, louder explosion of musket fire coming from both sides of the road. He spurred hard and sped forward, weaving in and out of panicked soldiers as he made his way toward Colonel Smith. Just as he came within sight of him, he saw the colonel suddenly lurch to one side in his saddle, then tumble out of it, hitting the ground heavily with one foot still in the stirrup.

Half a dozen men rushed forward to untangle him. Pitcarin saw blood flowing from a wound in his hip. The moans of pain mixed with the cacophony of musket fire, shouts, and running boots.

"Get him into the van and take care of the wound," he yelled to the men surrounding Smith, then waved them away and spun around to take command of the others.

"Return fire! Drive them back!" Turning to a captain of the grenadiers, he ordered loudly: "Get a company of your men and follow me into the farmyard!"

The company of twenty-five grenadiers rushed toward the small militia unit taking cover behind a stone wall protecting the farm ahead. There was a single cry of warning from the minutemen, then an explosion of flashes and a storm of musket balls. "Stand and fire!" Pitcarin screamed at his men, but before they had a chance to obey the order, four of them fell forward, dead or wounded. Swearing and squinting through the gun smoke, the major picked out one man, who appeared to be giving orders to the rest:

"That man in the blue coat! He's the officer! Aim for him!"

Seeing the British advancing, the small band suddenly scattered, but not before two fell—one of them the man in blue. As the grenadiers raced forward, their slender bayonets extended, the man in blue got to his knees and was dragged away by two comrades. The other wounded man, writhing in pain, remained where he lay on the ground.

"This'll ease the pain!" a grenadier yelled, as held his musket high over the man's head, then thrust the bayonet deep into his gut. Major Pitcarin, who witnessed the spectacle, looked away.

"Behind us, sir!" came a cry from Ensign DeBerniere. Looking over his shoulder, Pitcarin saw a large number of colonials coming toward them over the fields to their rear. He gave orders for the men in the farmyard to get back to the road and close ranks with the rest of the column. They obeyed, wearily, their feet dragging, the breath coming from their lungs in labored pants. Back on the road, the major looked west. Once more, the colonial muskets had taken their toll: more than a dozen regulars. He hoped for their sake they were dead, or close to it, because there would be no one going back to help.

13

He had walked, by his own estimate, a half mile along the Lexington Road, passing dead horses, dead and wounded men, and various British detritus, toward the cracking and popping of musket fire. The day had turned warm. The sun was high; Thompson could feel the heat rising along his legs from the road. Looking to the shrubbery on both sides, he thought he could see a faint greening: The buds on the bushes and trees would soon burst.

Suddenly he was overwhelmed with exhaustion. Coated in smoke and road dust, his throat burning from gunpowder and dryness, he felt—for all the weight of duty that pulled him toward the sounds of musket fire—that he simply must rest. There would be time, he told himself. He would miss little; the conflict would not be over today. Liberty, if it was to be, would be bought dearly, with months, even years of bloodshed. There would be time enough for one old soldier to take a minute's rest.

Leaning his musket against a moss-covered wall, he sat on the grassy berm and leaned back against the wall, sighing in relief. A small group of militiamen walked by him, headed west. So, he thought, there were still some going home. But there would be more to take their place.

He was slipping into a doze when he heard his name called: "Mr. Maxwell—it's you, isn't it, sir?"

Looking up, he saw that it was Jeremiah Fitch, a member of one of the Bedford militia companies.

"Are you hurt, sir?" Fitch inquired, polite, concerned.

"No, no, I'm fine. Just tired, bone-tired. But I'd have thought you and your men would be up with Captain Wilson by now."

"We should be, sir, but by the time we arrived at Concord, the fight was over. Then we became lost. We've been trying to catch up ever since. Do you know where the others are up there?" He gestured toward the firing. "We need our orders."

Up on his feet again, Thompson replied, "No, Sergeant, but let's move forward and perhaps we can find them. Jonathan and his men, I'm certain, are somewhere up ahead."

As they moved slowly toward Lexington, the noise of battle grew louder and the traffic of soldiers increased. After they had walked another half mile or so, Sergeant Fitch thought he spied a familiar face. "It's David Lane, sir, the Bedford fifer. That's him, I'm sure, in the blue jacket, coming this way!"

The boy was running, looking very anxious, scanning every face he passed. It was clear he was searching for someone. They were still twenty meters from each other when Sergeant Fitch waved his hat and called out: "David!"

David Lane stopped, looked around, then came running over. As he neared, Thompson couldn't help but be struck by the change he saw: A young boy of twelve or thirteen, he had arrived this morning with his fife at the muster, scrubbed clean as could be, the pride of any mother, clothes neat enough for church. Now he was as filthy and scruffy as the rest, with stained, ripped clothing, matted hair, and dirty face. He looked five years older, at least.

He stopped before them, panting. As he stood there, his face working—contorting—it slowly dawned on Thompson that David Lane was staring at him. A sense of dread invaded his heart. As quickly as that, the boy caught his breath and spoke. "Come quickly. Captain Wilson has been hurt."

Grasping his arm, Thompson, through his fatigue and panic, barely managed not to shout: "What happened? Where is he? Is he all right?"

"He's, he's alive, sir," the boy said. "We carried him to the farmhouse. He asked me to find you. You have to come quick, sir. Quick."

Thompson's heart was sinking as he and Fitch raced past the soldiers and stragglers, following David Lane. Minutes later, as they rounded a bend in the road, the young fifer pointed to a gray farm building and said: "He's in, sir. In there, on the table."

Entering, Thompson instantly recognized three men from the Bedford militia. One of them turned, recognized him just as quickly, and called out, "In here, Mr. Maxwell."

Jonathan was on a table. He was breathing; his blue coat moved up and down. He did not seem to be bleeding at the moment, though his shirt and coat were soaked in red. Dropping to his knees beside the table, Thompson placed his hand on Jonathan's head.

"Jonathan, Jonathan. I'm here."

His brother-in-law opened his eyes and, after a few seconds, Thompson thought he saw a flash of recognition. Then Jonathan opened his mouth, but what came out was too weak and muffled to be heard.

Thompson moved his ear closer to Jonathan's mouth. "Speak again, brother," he said doing his best to keep his voice calm and steady. "I couldn't quite make out what you said."

"Thompson, you old warrior." Jonathan breathed with an attempt at a smile. He was in obvious, terrible pain. "I should have heeded you, brother. We got too close. Foolish. . ." He took another slow breath. His hand moved to touch Thompson's. "Take care of the family. Please." He breathed out now with a hissing sound.

When Thompson replied, it was more a moan than a sentence: "I will, brother. I will."

Their hands were still together. But Thompson knew as he spoke that his words were no longer heard.

It took Thompson a week to reach the Amherst militia, encamped in Cambridge by the Charles River. They were long, endlessly long, painful days.

First, he had had to secure a wagon to bring Jonathan's body back to Bedford; most of the town attended the burial. Then he had to find someone to get his wagon, and the goods he'd left at Jonathan's, to Robert Means's store in Amherst, where he knew they would be safe.

But it was the walk from Bedford to Cambridge that was the worst. His thoughts would not leave Jonathan, and when they did, they were drawn to the memory of the young British fifer, the wounded boy he assumed was also dead. But mostly he thought of his brother-in-law: more than a brother-in-law, a patriot, a kindred spirit, a fine friend. The closest friend, probably, that Thompson Maxwell had ever had. And now he was gone.

One thing was certain, Thompson told himself as he walked. He would honor the promise he'd made to Jonathan: to care for his family, in whatever ways they required, for as long as necessary. Yet to do this, to honor this promise, he would have to survive these battles, he would have to keep himself safe.

He arrived in Cambridge, exhausted and filthy, on a Thursday afternoon. The city was teeming with militiamen, who, he learned, were encamped all around Boston, from Dorchester Heights to the beaches northeast of the city. Most, he thought, looked as tired and ragged as he.

He was directed to the campus of Harvard College, and from there to Cambridge Common, where, within minutes, he saw the men of the New Hampshire militia, including members of his own company, drilling on the green.

"Look! Look! It's Lieutenant Maxwell!" The cry went up as he made his way toward them. His hand was pumped repeatedly, his back thumped until he thought he could stand it no more.

"Where have you been?"

"We thought you were dead!"

"Did you join the British? There was a rumor they won you over with their food!"

Everyone's spirits seemed high, notwithstanding all the questions. Thompson assured them he would give a detailed account soon enough. But first, he said, he must report to Captain Crosby. Young Thomas Powell, the drummer, volunteered to lead him there.

In the vine-covered academic building where the New Hampshire militia, for the moment, was based, Captain Crosby welcomed him, as did the other officers, though Thompson thought he detected a ripple of surprised discomfort as he walked into the room.

The amenities ended, he gave his account: the rout at Concord, the retreat to Lexington, Jonathan's death, the delivery of his body to Bedford.

When he had finished, the captain came around the table he'd been standing behind to clasp Thompson's arm.

"I am deeply sorry for your loss, Thompson. Captain Wilson was a fine man and an excellent soldier. He will be missed."

Then he cleared his throat, looking a little uncomfortable.

"I do not like to tell you this, but it seems your return was doubted, especially when it was delayed so long. No one had realized, of course, where you had been, although we suspected you had been involved. But then there was the further absence. We couldn't have known the delay was because you were bringing your brother-in-law's body home."

Thompson looked from Crosby to the others, searching the faces for some sign of what might be coming.

"It's understandable, sir," he said. "None of us know's who may fall, who may not return after a battle. I could easily have been among those killed."

Crosby shook his head and continued. "Ambitious men are sometimes a plague on the military, Thompson."

Thompson returned the captain's look with a small grimace of confusion.

"By that you mean—?"

"Most, including myself, did not lose hope of your return. We know what a fine, seasoned soldier you are. At the same time, however, there were some who were counting on your not coming back. I, I tell you this only because you are sure to hear of it from the men."

"I'm not following you, sir."

"Sergeants Mills and Sawyer, I'm afraid, have spent much of the past two days campaigning for votes among the company—to succeed you as lieutenant."

Thompson bit his tongue as he felt the red rising in his face.

"By what authority—"

"Thompson, I need not tell you how glad I am of your safe return. I know, too, that all present here feel the same."

Crosby stopped, smiled warmly, and put his arm on Thompson's shoulder.

"Now is not the time to worry about these matters. You have fought a hard campaign, you have just buried a friend. You are tired, and deservedly so. You need a rest."

"Sir, I—"

"Please know this, Thompson. Your experience and abilities are valued, and will be needed soon enough. You have nothing to concern yourself about."

With that, the captain motioned to Drummer Powell.

"Escort Lieutenant Maxwell to the very best room we have. Goodnight, Thompson. We will talk again when you are fresh."

14

AMHERST
APRIL 20, 1775

THE RINGING OF THE BELL, the tapping of the drum, and the shrill notes of the fife were everywhere in the village. It was the largest crowd Joshua Atherton had ever seen on Amherst Common. Not even the raising of the second meetinghouse had brought out such numbers—and that had featured free rum.

Clusters of citizens stood around the common, talking to members of the militia and to one another. Most spectators seemed to belong to one of two general groups. The first was largely women—wives and mothers, weeping and consoling each other in advance for the awful losses they feared from the war that had begun yesterday. Some were holding tight to their loved ones, fearful that this could be their last time together.

The second group, nearly all men, seemed interested only in trading and gathering news: everyone talking at once of the attacks by the British, two days before, on Lexington and Concord. Most had never heard of the two Massachusetts towns, and were inquiring of each other where they were in relation to Amherst.

To Joshua, yesterday, April 19, seemed a year ago, but a day he could never forget. He had been in the county building on Jailhouse

Road, busy at his duties as registrar of probate—which consisted of reviewing county files—when he was been startled by the firing of guns, followed immediately by the ringing of the town's only bell.

"The British have attacked Concord, Massachusetts! All the militia from Massachusetts have joined together. They are fighting the British! It has begun!"

It was Daniel Wilkins Jr., all but hysterical on the common outside.

The county building emptied like water from a bottomless bucket. Everyone headed for the meetinghouse, where Jabez Holt, the fifer from Captain Crosby's militia company, was already ringing the bell. Captain Crosby stood on the doorstep, repeating to the gathering numbers the very few facts he knew. The questions flew around him like buzzing gnats: "How many colonials have been killed in the fighting?" "How did it begin?" "How far away is Lexington?" "What do you think will happen next?"

Joshua had stood alone at the outskirts, watching and listening. After a few minutes, he had looked up to see Robert Means at his side.

"I wonder how real this can seem to them," Means said quietly. "How many do you know in Amherst who have ever set foot out of town, much less Hillsborough County? For all most of them know, it might as well be happening on the moon."

The pain Joshua felt was almost physical. "Distance will not help us, Robert. It will not keep us safe. The wrath of King George, the might of his military, they will be upon us. We will look back on the French War as nothing."

"Come, Joshua, you give us little credit. We have the strength of a new nation; all King George has is paid soldiers. And poorly paid, at that. How hard will men like that fight, compared to those fighting for their homes, their families, their liberty?"

"Yes, Robert. And the men of Scotland were fighting for their homes not even thirty years ago, and look what George II did to them. Murdered most of the men and boys after the battle of Culloden."

Joshua pointed to the stocks and whipping post near by. "We punish our own offenders, too often brutally. What punishment will the king visit on us, do you think, the perpetrators of revolution?"

Captain Crosby, standing apart, was still answering questions. "I have told you all I know!" he bellowed, becoming impatient now. "My commander, Colonel Shepard, has called for the Amherst militia to assemble here at dawn tomorrow. From here we will march to Cambridge. That's all I know and all I can say."

The next morning, April 21, Joshua and Abigail arrived at the common at a few minutes past dawn. The militia was assembling already—one hundred men, with muskets and provisions, in criss-crossing columns on the grass.

Abigail had wept through much of the night. Now, standing on the common in the dim dawn light, looking out over the assembled militia, she issued a muffled moan as she began again to weep. Joshua put his arm around her and held her tightly to him, knowing as he did that his comfort was small at best.

"Yesterday, it was us I was crying for—you and me, the children. This morning I see how selfish I was. Look, look"—she made a sweeping gesture that took in the whole of the common—"most of them are not more than children, going off to fight, perhaps to die. Look there, Joshua. There's Jebez Holt, the fifer. He can't be more than fourteen years old!"

Looking up, Joshua saw the thin, almost frail boy and remembered how conscientiously the lad had performed chores around the law office this past spring. Jebez wanted to be a lawyer. A wave of sadness flowed over him as he was torn by the thought of death or injury awaiting the small boy. As much as to comfort himself, Joshua took Abigail's hand and turned gently to face her: "We must be strong, Abigail. We must be strong." It was all he could think of to say.

Just at that moment, on the steps in front of the meetinghouse, the young fifer, Jebez Holt, and the drummer, Thomas Powell, sounded the call to assembly. Immediately the small militia formed itself in companies facing the steps. Mr. Wilkins, who had been moving among groups for the last several minutes, mounted the steps and turned to face the militia, and the citizens who stood to their backs.

The crowd quieted. The minister asked God's blessing "in the coming struggle," and prayed that he would "keep our young men safe." More than once, Joshua noticed him glance fleetingly toward his own son, Daniel, who was standing in the front row.

Abigail was right, Joshua thought—they were mostly boys. The last census, he recalled, listed 328 males in Amherst over the age of sixteen. Nearly a third would march to Massachusetts this day, a hundred young males who would otherwise be tilling, planting crops, helping their fathers and brothers manage Amherst's shops and stores—much of which would now be women's work.

Joshua had been to Portsmouth often and to Boston once or twice, and had witnessed British troops on parade. They were an impressive sight, immaculate in their red dress uniforms and shiny steel weapons, marching with a crispness and precision that was almost a pleasure to watch. What a contrast to the motley little group he saw before him now, no two men or boys in the same set of clothes, some in field outfits, others in Sunday best, still others in hybrids of the two. Each soldier had his own musket at least, though even these were mismatched. Most were fowling pieces; the rest dated to the French War, twenty years before, and had probably been obsolete then. As for the officers' swords, heavy and formless, some forged by local blacksmiths, they would have served more use on the farm.

"Oh Abigail." The wail escaped his lips before he could check it. "How can a troop of farmers and shopkeepers hope to survive against the king's army?"

His wife's reply was immediate. "You are underestimating their spirit, Joshua. Your intellect gets in the way of common sense. You become blind. We, and our parents before us, have forged a new country and want only to be masters of it. Who is to say we cannot?"

Joshua stared at his wife in amazement. Her chin was high, her eyes shining, free of tears, as she viewed the lines of men. She looked proud, almost like a parent, he thought.

Slowly, to the sounds of drum and fife and the roar of the crowd at their back, the Amherst militia began its long march south along the Boston Post Road toward Cambridge. For a while, small children ran after them and alongside, shouting and cheering. Then the children fell away as their parents called them back, and small family groups began their lingering retreat from the common, which was nearly silent now and would empty soon enough.

Joshua and Abigail began their own walk home, both alone with their thoughts. As they made their way back along Courthouse Road, neither one speaking, Joshua had a sudden, half-panicked thought: For most of the past hour, the families on the common, many of them neighbors, some of them old friends, had been milling about, talking, gossiping, exchanging news. Yet almost none approached him or Abigail. And those who did remained only long enough to be polite. Was it his imagination? Was this what it was like to be shunned?

He looked around as they walked. In a nearby group, he caught the eye of a farmer named Eustus, a man about his own age who lived nearby, who quickly looked away. He had a brief flash of his exchanges of a year ago: with Robert Means, then Daniel Wilkins, on their way together down Mack Hill. Both men had warned him; both warnings he'd dismissed.

He felt a cloud settle over his heart. He glanced sideways at his wife. She did not see him, or if she did she did not let him know. At least for the moment, the two were together but alone.

Robert Means House and Store

Robert Means and his sons operated a general store on this site well into
the nineteenth century. It was in this house that Robert Means's granddaughter married the future president Franklin Pierce in 1834.

15

AMHERST
SUMMER 1775

"Joshua, you don't listen! You're too much the idealist. That intellect of yours, it's no friend to you sometimes. For God's sakes, man, be sensible! The war has started. It's too late for compromise!"

Joshua Atherton and Robert Means, as they did so many mornings lately, were standing in the back of Means's store just south of Amherst Common, debating the wisdom of the colonials' fight with the king. Robert was finding himself increasingly exasperated with his friend: Joshua seemed almost constitutionally unable to adjust his views to reality. He talked continually of the importance of "simple reason" and argued without end that the colonists' only recourse was to "compromise their high ideals" and "sue for peace." If the revolution were to continue, he predicted, the colonies would be "crushed like ants underfoot" by the massive British army.

Joshua smiled; he knew his friend was truly agitated this morning. A sure sign of his temper was when, as now, a hint of his Irish heritage showed in his voice, an accent Means struggled to expel. "Not good for business," he would reply when chided by Joshua.

This morning's exchange, then, was running its usual heated course when Robert suddenly trailed off in mid-sentence and looked toward the front of the store, from which came the sounds of foot-steps and a door banging closed.

"Good morning to you, Robert!"

It was Paul Dudley Sargent, member of the Committee of Safety and one of Amherst's delegates to the New Hampshire Provincial Congress.

Sargent's tone cooled quickly as he eyed Robert's guest. "Oh yes, Attorney Atherton," he said and then pointedly, with an unmistakable trace of disdain, "am I interrupting something here?"

"Not at all," replied the always good-natured Robert. "In fact, you can add to the conversation. We were discussing the intricacies of New Hampshire government."

Sargent had been among the firebrands in the New Hampshire Assembly, the legislative body that had operated with the blessings of the king and Governor Wentworth until it was "dissolved" last year when it had refused to abide by the governor's order that it end its contacts with the other colonies. In defiance of the governor, the members reconvened in Exeter, called itself the New Hampshire Provincial Congress, and boasted of being "the people's government." For a while it had coexisted with the governor's legislative body in Portsmouth; now, with the revolution under way, it was the de facto authority in the state, with most of the towns in New Hampshire being represented. Sargent was one of the delegates from Amherst

Joshua, feeling the effects of Sargent's iciness, backed slowly toward the door.

"I'll let the two of you talk. Abigail is expecting me home, in any event."

"Take her my best wishes," Robert told him.

Sargent simply nodded and turned away. Then, as soon as the door closed behind Joshua, Sargent faced the storekeeper once again. "Robert, Robert, I know that you like and respect Atherton; I understand he is your friend. And no one could fault you for loyalty to friends, but in this case you do yourself no good."

He paused briefly to look at Robert, to measure the effects of his words, then continued: "Our congress has met in Exeter. I have been instructed to return and speak with you."

Robert was plainly flustered. "About what? What would they want with me, a storekeeper, a merchant?"

"Ah," Sargent said with a smile. "You underestimate yourself, Robert. You have the respect of the citizens of Amherst and of the surrounding communities, not only as a successful merchant and member of the community, but as a patriot as well."

Robert was uncomfortable. He was not close to Sargent; there was no cause for such flattery. As he opened his mouth, uncertain what to answer, the sound of the front door opening announced the arrival of a customer. Grateful for the diversion, Robert excused himself, took his time with the small transaction, then returned. Sargent didn't seem inclined to leave.

"I apologize, Paul," said Robert. All of my men are out delivering supplies. I am left to tend to the customers alone."

"Please, don't apologize. I'll come right to the point. Your name was brought forth yesterday, as a possible member of the Committee of Safety for Hillsborough County. With the war started, it is urgent that we organize now, and carry out the provisions of our charter— the preservation of peace and good order, the rooting out of subversives in our midst."

Robert stared at Sargent. He thought he understood now.

"If you are suggesting my taking action against Joshua, no, sir, I will not consider it!" His voice rose as anger filled him. "Look what your committees are doing to so many good men, driving them from their homes, inquisitions, threats of imprisonment. All in the name of that motto you have—how does it go exactly? 'Resistance to tyranny becomes the Christian and social duty of each individual.' Have I got it right?"

Now it was Sargent's turn to retreat. He had not expected such a reaction from the always cordial Means.

"Robert, please understand. There are British spies everywhere, men who want the revolution to fail. They are a danger to New Hampshire. We must safeguard the rights and privileges of the citizens of our state."

Means felt his temper cooling, as it nearly always did after the initial outburst. He took a deep breath. There was nothing to gain in angering Sargent, who, after all, was an influential man, and no chance that he would change his views. The best course, he thought, was to bring this meeting to a quick and amicable end.

He was silent for a moment, then spoke: "I understand your concerns, and the need for vigilance. But we must be fair, must we not, sir, as well as vigilant, if we are to have a people's government and not merely some new form of tyranny? Is it not important that we honor the freedom of our citizens to express their views?"

Sargent's face was stony. Means felt some of his courage seeping away; he did not wish to risk being judged a Loyalist himself, the consequences to his family and property would be disastrous. Then, before he could check himself, he heard his own voice blurt out: "Yes, I will consider your inquiry, sir. I will give it careful thought."

Sargent looked taken aback, then suddenly careful. It occurred to Robert in that instant that he was perhaps neither as powerless nor as inconsequential as he had supposed. He had been approached as a wealthy merchant, and one with influence in Amherst and throughout the county. The congress would be needing the support of citizens such as himself.

"Thank you, sir. I return to Exeter tomorrow. I will carry back your response."

Sargent started toward the door, then stopped abruptly and turned.

"Robert, I share your concern of trading one villain for another. Please be assured, there are men among us already working on a new constitution for the state. A citizens' government. Dr. Matthew Thornton of Londonderry, Benjamin Giles of Newport, Meshech

Weare of Hampton Falls, Judge Wyseman Claggett of Litchfield. And others, good men all. Ours will be a government of the people. Be assured of it." With that, he turned and left the store.

Means stood still a full minute, staring at the boards of the shop's floor. He was thinking about war, about how it felt sometimes that there were two wars happening—the first against the king over sovereignty, the other among the colonists themselves.

He made a mental promise to himself: to meet in private with his friends in the future, to bear in mind the truth of what was said—that a man is known by the company he keeps.

16

CAMBRIDGE COMMON
JUNE 17, 1775

THE SOUND OF THUNDER rolled over the Harvard College campus.

"What the hell!" exclaimed young Daniel Wilkins, stopping in his tracks in the hallway of Stoughton Hall, bringing up his hands involuntarily to cover his head before lowering them slowly in embarrassment. He turned to face Thompson. "That's cannon fire!" he said.

Wilkins, the other lieutenant in Thompson's militia company, was young enough never to have heard the sounds of rolling cannon fire in the distance. The dull booming rattled the building shutters. Thompson nodded and held up his hand up for silence, listening. His first thought was that it was merely a morning salute; then, as he made out the frequency, coupled with the differences in tone, he knew differently:

"That's British cannon!" he said. "We don't have that many guns, nor the powder to waste."

He went down the stairs, Wilkins at his side. The two men ran out the door of Stoughton Hall, nearly colliding with an officer from another company, who then joined them. The three men trotted toward regimental headquarters.

Like an anthill under siege, the Harvard College buildings were emptying—officers clustering in loud little groups, enlisted men running to their drill or breakfast sites, all anxious to learn what was going on.

Thompson felt almost grateful. The past two months—since the events at the bridge at Concord—had been unspeakably dull. The only activity consisted of the daily drilling, followed at night by either drinking in the Cambridge taverns or the do-nothing boredom of sentry duty. Most of the enlisted men had run out of money, due largely to overspending on drink. Some had simply left and walked home; others wanted to—it was planting time, and they felt useless here. It had begun to seem, for many, that the adventure was at an end. Now, perhaps, it would be different, Thompson thought.

As they reached the regimental headquarters of Colonel Reed, Adjutant Stephen Peabody was giving orders to the runners. All companies except officers, who were to meet with Colonels Stark and Reed at Harvard Hall, were to muster, in full gear, at their drill site on Cambridge Common.

The flurry of inquiries went on unabated as officers continued to arrive. Turning to leave, Thompson noticed Colonel Stark, who shared command with Colonel Reed, emerge from a room just down the hall. Thompson gestured a greeting to the tall, strong-featured man, wondering what response, if any, he would get.

Stark started down the hallway, caught sight of Thompson, hesitated a second, then stopped dead: "I know you! You were with me at Fort Ticonderoga!"

Thompson felt a glow of pride warm his chest. Both men had served in Rogers's Rangers, Stark as an officer, Thompson as a foot soldier—a boy of fifteen. As young as he was, he had given all he had, and he knew the officers had valued him.

"Yes, sir," he said now. "And at Fort George and Crown Point. I am Thompson Maxwell, now lieutenant in the Amherst militia, under Colonel Reed."

Stark laughed. "What a long time it's been, but I knew I recognized the face. We're going to need some seasoned veterans today. I'm happy to see you here."

He grasped Thompson's arm and squeezed it, then turned and walked through the front door, a group of officers soon surrounding him.

Daniel Wilkins, impressed, asked excitedly, "You know Colonel Stark?"

"We fought together, for three years, in the French War. He'll lead us well. He's a brave, determined man. But never mind that. Let's get back to Stoughton, for our equipment. Then on to Harvard Hall."

Fifteen minutes later, at a little before nine in the morning, the two officers, along with several dozen others, were part of a raucous cluster outside Harvard Hall. For another ten minutes or so, the group milled about impatiently, exchanging gossip and information, listening to the continuing dull thunder of the cannon in the distance.

Then Colonels Stark and Reed arrived. The officers crowded tightly around them. When the silence was near total, Stark began: "In May Colonel Putnam recognized the importance of fortifying heights in Charlestown. He urged the Massachusetts Bay Committee of Safety to approve his plan to mount cannon on Bunker Hill and barrage Boston and the warships in the harbor, but they rejected the plan as being too aggressive considering the meager supply of gunpowder we possess. Two days ago the committee received news that General Gage planned to attack Cambridge through Charlestown and reconsidered Putnam's plan. The Committee of Safety passed a resolution on June 13 authorizing the fortification of Bunker Hill.

"You saw the Massachusetts companies leave yesterday at twilight, with Colonel Prescott in command.

"When Colonel Prescott arrived on the Charlestown peninsula, he found that Bunker Hill was too far back to serve as an effective cannon site. He chose to fortify Breeds Hill instead; it's higher and nearer the shore. By moonlight and starlight, the eight hundred militia from Massachusetts and Connecticut, armed with picks and shovels, constructed a three-sided earthen fortress with gunports ready for our cannon. We now command the heights above Boston and the harbor."

"Whose cannon do we hear?" came a call from one officer. "Surely we don't have that number of guns."

"No, we don't. We had hoped General Gage would take no action for the time being, but when the British saw the fortress, their ships in the harbor and the guns on Copps Hill in Boston were ordered to fire on it.

"I estimate there are two hundred cannons, but at the time of the last message, there has been no damage to our fort. It is holding up well and our comrades are uninjured."

"That's farmers for you!" bellowed someone in the crowd. "One thing we know how to do is dig!"

The colonel smiled briefly, then continued. His voice, it seemed to Thompson, took on new gravity. "It's important you men understand this," he said. "British pride is at stake. They cannot—they will not—allow that fort, a symbol of our resistance, to stare them in the face. They will attack. And when they do, our left flank—the land between the fort and the Mystic River to the east—will be wide open, defenseless. They could, with relative ease, flank the fort, surround it, capture the few guns we have there, and massacre eight hundred men.

"Eight hundred are not enough to withstand the British numbers. Therefore, men, your orders: The New Hampshire militia will fortify and defend the left flank."

A cheer went up from every officer in the group. Hats were thrown high in the air. Colonel Stark held up his hands to quell the din: "The time for celebration is later. There is a fortress—and eight hundred lives—to defend. Return to your companies, and prepare them to march by ten."

General Gage was still in bed when the frigate *Lively* commenced firing its ten starboard cannon at dawn that day.

"My gown! Where is my gown!" He bellowed for his steward.

Still, Gage was not a man to be rushed. He washed, then donned his robe with relative calm. By the time he was dressed, the cannon barrage had expanded to broadsides from half the British warships in the harbor. The thundering of guns shook Province House, rattling its windows and shutters, as, he imagined, it did most other buildings in Boston.

It was his plan to climb to the roof to determine the direction of the firing. But before he could leave his bedchamber, an aide arrived with the news: A crude rebel fortress had been erected during the night on a hill in Charlestown.

He dressed hastily—as hastily as he did anything—swearing several times under his breath, pausing only long enough to order runners to fetch Generals Howe, Clinton, and Burgoyne.

The three generals had arrived in Boston only a week after the disasters at Concord and Lexington, yet each seemed to style himself an instant expert on the conflict. Clinton's view, especially, made the general see red. He had heard it too many times already, in the days that led up to Concord and the loss of four hundred of his men: "Show them the bayonet, and you'll see the cowards run." It had proved wrong then, it maddened him now.

On his way up the stairs to the roof to get a view of the harbor, it occurred to him suddenly that he had neglected to summon the most critical figure of all. He called for his aide yet again.

"Please extend my best wishes to Admiral Graves, and ask if he would be so kind as to join us."

The aide's eyebrows rose, though only the barest fraction. Graves had been a thorn in the general's side for well over a year. As the sole commander of the British fleet, he seemed sometimes to use his authority just remind others that he was free to do as he pleased. It could only have been Graves who had ordered the cannon fire today.

The general had been on the roof barely a minute when he realized that he could just as well have left his telescope behind—the damned colonists were that close, their earth fortress and clots of men easily visible with the naked eye. By the time he descended for his meeting, and shook the hands of Howe, Clinton, and Burgoyne, he was as agitated as he had been in weeks.

Each of the generals, predictably, offered his own version of how the day should go, though each with reasonable deference to his commander—for which he was grateful. Twenty minutes into the meeting, with neither warning nor knock, the double doors burst open, admitting the portly, red-faced Admiral Graves. General Gage, briefly surprised, offered a curt but genial greeting. But Graves, apparently in a state of pique at being summoned on such short notice, was in no mood for amenities. "I told you in May to burn Charlestown," he said.

The general did his best to stay calm. But the admiral wasn't through: "If you had done that, and told these farmers it would happen to every one of their towns, they would have been on their knees to you by now."

Gage held tight to his restraint: "Yes, Admiral, you may have been right. But now we have a different matter to resolve. Let us try to work in harmony. Time grows short."

Muttering, the admiral lowered his bulk into a chair. He was mercifully silent for several minutes.

The discussion, heated at times, went on for nearly an hour. Clinton's recommendation was to assault both sides of the thin strip of land that joined Charlestown to the mainland—the Charles River basin on the west and the Mystic River on the east. This would cut off the colonial retreat to the mainland. Gage's instinct was to reject this idea outright; he possessed too little knowledge of the colonists' strength and the last thing he needed was for his landing force to be attacked from two sides—Charlestown and Boston. But before he could manage more than the briefest of replies, Clinton interrupted, apparently not yet through. He seemed in love with his words: "The fort is just a pimple on Breeds Hill. We can isolate and starve them into surrender with just few casualties on our side."

It was Graves who spoke now, his deep voice a rumble: "You may suffer few casualties on the ground, but I don't have the proper landing boats for that water. Your men will drown in the heavy surf before they reach the Mystic River shore or in the deep mud in the shallow Charles River basin."

Clinton stared, for once at a loss for words.

"Thank you, Admiral." Gage spoke quietly in the sudden silence. "Furthermore, we don't know the colonials' strength on the mainland. Remember Concord. We cannot take a chance on being squeezed between two forces."

The commander stood and began to pace the room, musing aloud.

"No. The slope of Breeds Hill is gradual on the sides facing Boston and the Mystic River, and the fortress—we will call it that for the moment—is just a pit and a mound of dirt. We can make a frontal attack up the gradual slope, meanwhile maneuvering around their flank, along the Mystic River shore, then attacking from the rear."

It was General How's turn to speak. He had been silent up to now.

Of the five of them, he may have been the veteran of the most campaigns.

"The general is correct." There was a dissenting grumble from Clinton, which Howe cut off with a wave of his arm. "Remember, gentlemen, I was born here. I know these people. They are like children, spoiled children. Give them an inch and they'll scream for a yard. Theirs is a tantrum that will not cease if we suffer it willingly by being soft on them. General Gage is right. We must hammer them with maximum strength and leave no chance for response."

"Yes, yes," put in General Burgoyne, smacking his hand on the table for emphasis. "Make it a bayonet charge. There's nothing like the blade to get them running."

He laughed uproariously at own joke, with Clinton joining in at the end. General Gage opened his mouth to speak, but Clinton was off again. "These colonials, they fight as only cowards fight, from behind rocks and trees. They deserve the worst we can deliver. Give them the blade."

His voice rose as he spoke, competing with the increased noise of shelling from the direction of Copp's Hill. Gage did not bother to compete. He took a step toward the group of officers, raised his hand for silence, and waited for General Clinton to comply.

"It is decided," said Gage. "Our force will land on the southernmost point of the peninsula, from where a two-pronged attack will be made—frontally, up the slope in front of the fortress, together with a flanking move along the shore to attack it from the rear.

"We will use two thousand grenadiers and light infantry to storm the fort, with a company of marines in reserve. There will be no chances taken of being outnumbered. The command will go to General Howe."

Admiral Graves agreed that sufficient transport would be made available: twenty-eight barges, each large enough to ferry fifty men to the landing area at Moulton's Point, a safe half mile from the fort. General Howe expressed some concern as to the safety of landing at low tide; it was agreed to wait until two in the afternoon, when the tide would again be coming in.

As General Howe stood to leave, Gage grasped his arm and in a firm, almost threatening voice said, "General, as the king's representative, responsible for all the colonies, I want you to understand the political importance of your command. You have the opportunity today to stop the rebels before they gain strength. Understand, not only the peace of these colonies is at stake. If any idea were to spread that this revolution was successful, it could encourage insurrection in Canada, the West Indies, even Ireland. No, we must check this now, for good."

Howe could only mutter, "I understand and will succeed," then he abruptly turned and walked from the room with his aide, Abijah

Willard, to see to the preparation of his troops. He would give orders for the grenadiers and light-infantry units to pack a three-day supply of food and materiel and assemble at the wharf.

The fact that the colonists would now have many more hours to prepare did not seem to disturb him. Nor did the fact that each British foot soldier would be carrying more than hundred pounds of equipment uphill in the summer heat. There would be nothing the rebels could do, he told himself, to stop his troops' charge. He wondered if they would even try, against such an awesome force.

"These colonials have never seen our like," he said to Abijah, smiling thinly. "The British army will be like a red tidal wave engulfing the beach."

17

CHARLESTOWN NECK

THOMPSON WAS PLEASED with the Amherst militia's preparations, considering the limits imposed. Each man had been issued one cup of powder, one flint, and enough lead to form fifteen balls for the widely varying musket calibers. (The lead had been taken from the organ pipes of a Cambridge church.) Although fifteen balls was too meager to be adequate, most of the Amherst men had some extras from their personal supplies. Even so, powder and shot would be in short supply.

Their gear assembled, they were instructed to muster on the common with a full canteen and whatever food they could gather. No delays would be allowed; soldiers not present would be left behind.

In less than an hour the Amherst company was ready; not a single man missed the call.

For the four miles from Cambridge to Charlestown, the regiments marched to the beat of pounding drums. Thompson could see that the men were enjoying themselves. The feeling was festive, anticipatory; children danced and cheered alongside; men and women hung out from windows offering encouragement: "Give them a musket ball for me." "Send them all to hell!" "Cheers for New Hampshire!" At one group of buildings, a dozen young boys began

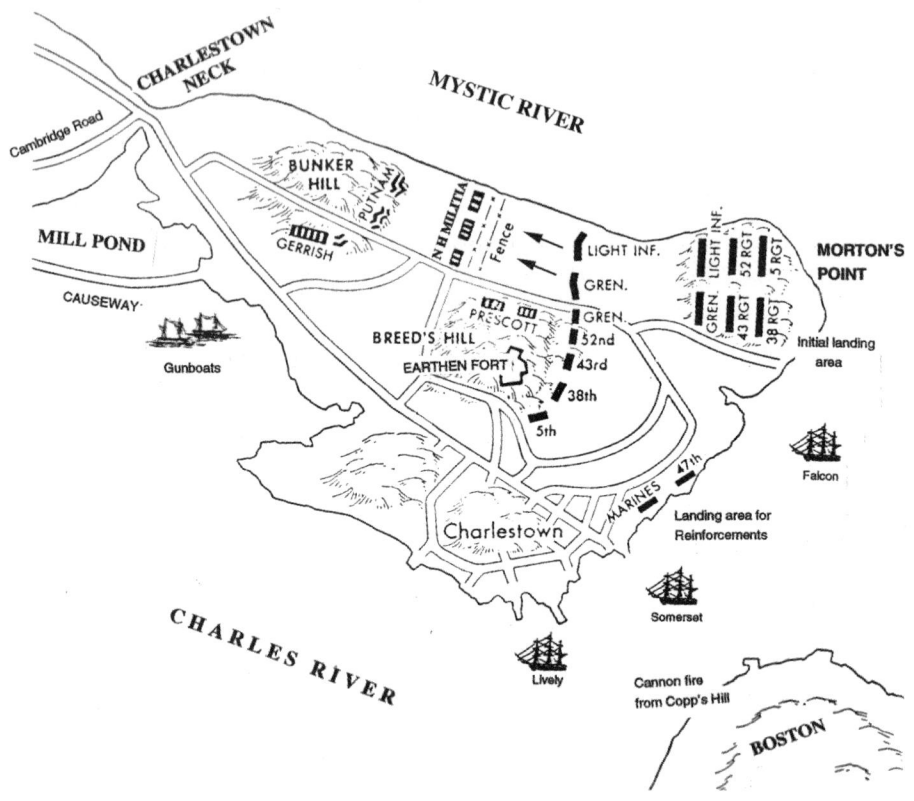

Map of Charlestown Peninsula and the British Attack.

to shout a tuneless *Yankee Doodle*. Thompson could see the pride in the men's faces. He felt proud himself.

As the company approached Charlestown Neck, he could hear the sharp bark of small cannon, close at hand, mixed with the dull, distant roar of the larger guns rolling toward them from the other side of the Charlestown hills. As the Neck came into view, he was able to make out a six small British gunboats anchored in the shallows, firing on the colonists trying to make their way across.

Charlestown, shaped like a teardrop, is connected to the mainland by the tiniest sliver of land—the Neck. All traffic to and from the village must pass over this, which, at high tide, is only barely passable in an ordinary wagon. The British gunboats were anchored in the bay west of the marsh and swamp—as close as they could get without running aground.

Captain Crosby called a halt and took Thompson and Daniel Wilkins aside.

"The company will be exposed to fire from the gunboats for about a quarter mile as we cross Charlestown Neck. Then we will have the cover of small hills until we reach Breeds Hill. Thank God the warships can't get into the bay."

"It doesn't look as though the fire is too effective; there are men crossing," Wilkins said.

"Yes, all but the unlucky ones," answered Crosby. "When we reach the mainland side of the Neck you'll see the casualties— Colonel Stark has ordered that the bodies of those fallen be hidden from view, to keep the others from losing heart. But we could not get to all of them; there are still some lying along the path, just before we come into range of the guns."

Thompson and Daniel Wilkins both nodded. Then Thompson had an added thought: "Sir, few of the men in our company have witnessed wartime death. We will push them swiftly, to keep them from reacting overmuch to what they see before they are out of range. I might even suggest, sir, that we have them cross in quick-time."

"No!" Captain Crosby's face reddened. Thompson was taken aback. Perhaps, Thompson thought, his quick anger could be masking something else—fear, nervousness, or a loss of confidence. He kept silent and waited for what would come next.

"Colonel Stark crossed the Neck at a walk," Crosby said, in a markedly calmer tone. "He too was encouraged to run the men over; his response was that one fresh man in action is worth ten too tired to fight. I agree. We, like him, will cross at a walk."

As they approached the narrow passage, the spectacle that Crosby had described came into view, bloody and vivid. Some of the men balked, even stopped, and had to be prodded from behind. Several turned to retch at the sight; Thompson could hear snatches of prayer and low moans. Still, for all that, the column kept moving, in an almost orderly fashion, with Wilkins and Thompson offering all of the encouragement they could. Shot from the shallow draft gunboats splashed all around them in the shallow bay, sometimes landing with dull thumps in the nearby sandy soil.

The men were like nervous horses, Thompson thought, trying to keep to the path, facial muscles flinching in fear as they tried not to give in to the panic they felt, forcing their eyes straight ahead. Most terrifying of all, to him, was the sound of shot skipping over water: a high, whizzing noise, allowing just enough time for those listening to wonder where it would hit, before the thud that marked its harmless demise in the sand. The British aim, for the most part, was poor, no doubt owing to the choppy waves in the bay, which caused the boats to rise and fall with the swells.

Suddenly, there was a different sound—a loud, swishing, high-pitched noise like a scream on the wind. It ended in a thud similar to that of the shot, but not quite the same. Thompson heard Wilkins yell next to him, his voice near panic.

"They're firing lengths of chain!"

Thompson gathered himself quickly, then shouted up and down the line: "It sounds worse than it is! Keep moving!"

It was not true, and he knew it. He could do nothing more, though, but to keep a tight rein on his own fear and see that the men moved forward as swiftly as possible. Damn Crosby, he thought, for forcing us to walk.

From somewhere ahead, Thompson heard a scream, then men yelling. Running forward, he pushed his way past the marchers in front of him before rounding a corner and bumping into a small knot of men clustered around a slumped figure. It was young Peter Robinson, a private, moaning and holding his right wrist with his left hand. As tight as his grip was—his knuckles were as white as bed-sheets—the blood continued to spurt from the arm at an extraordinary rate, spitting onto the clothes of the men who stood around him.

"Tie a cord or rope around the arm to stop the bleeding," Thompson said to one of them, who seemed to be a friend. "The rest of you, keep moving!"

He tried to keep his voice subdued, soldierly, but he was staring at the boy's arm, which ended at the wrist. The hand was gone, carried away by a cannonball. It could have been a chain length, he thought, and a lot more than a hand. He reached down and gripped the private firmly under one arm and raised him to his feet.

Panic was close at hand; there was no disputing it. Thompson steeled himself to be pitiless the rest of the way. A hundred more yards, he thought, and we'll be out of range of the guns.

Two men, Jonathan Small and Alexander Brown, had stopped dead in their tracks in their march past Robinson, and were standing next to him, shaking like leaves in a wind.

"You two," Thompson commanded, "help carry him back to the mainland for care, and keep the wrist straight up—don't let it bleed again. And I want to see you both back here!"

He ground out the last words, more from a wish to motivate the men than from any belief that they would be seen again today.

At last they reached the cover of the hillside, and Thompson was able to survey his surroundings. Up ahead, on what must be Breeds Hill, he saw the back of the earthen fort the Massachusetts militia had dug the night before. The hill showed a steep slope from the fort toward the town of Charlestown on the right.

"Well, at least the right flank is secure," he said bitterly, turning to Wilkins. "Charlestown is on fire."

"The British must have set fire to it," replied Wilkins.

Thompson looked ahead, toward the thick black clouds of smoke billowing from the burning buildings. He thought he had never seen smoke so thick or so dark; it seemed to blot out the sun.

"The bastards," Wilkins said.

As they climbed to a point between the two hills, he gained a closer view of the fortress they had been told about earlier that day: Crudely made and three-sided, it was open in the rear.

He considered this carefully: While it commanded a strategic position, an ideal site, it was clearly vulnerable to attack from the rear. Half a mile of gradual slope separated it from the Mystic River shore—it would be an easy matter for the British to march around the fort, out of musket range of the defenders inside, and attack from the back.

Just then he caught sight of Captain Crosby, who was coming their way on the run: "The British are ferrying troops across from Boston," Crosby panted out, all but spent from his effort. "The New Hampshire militia has been ordered to fortify the left flank from the fortress to the shore. Our area is over there."

Crosby pointed to a section of low stone wall.

"Colonel Stark has ordered fences, rocks, even piles of cut hay"— he gestured toward some haystacks in the nearby fields—"to be stacked so that to the British our positions will appear to be a secure barricade."

Thompson wondered how he would manage to put this command in a positive, even plausible light for his already terrified men.

"We don't have much time," he heard Crosby snap.

Thompson nodded quickly, understanding his mission, and walked toward the Amherst men. He would stay calm, he told himself, even if that was all he managed to do. He wondered briefly if ever, in all his years in the military, he had been in a position more absurd or hopeless than this. He thought not.

The sound of cannon fire was deafening, but fortunately directed toward the fort and not at them. Then he saw the reason why. The British assembly point was on the shore in front of them, less than a mile away, straight in the path of a poorly aimed shot. Through the smoke of the cannon fire drifting over the water, he saw a continuous stream of barges—each with fifty or more men—arriving from Boston to the beach below them. By his guess, there were more than a thousand men gathered there already, with other barges visible on the water behind.

"They don't seem in a hurry to attack. They seem to be having an afternoon meal," said one of the soldiers near Thompson.

By pushing, ordering, and cajoling, but mostly by working beside the men, Thompson and Wilkins motivated the company to gather piles of rocks, brush, and timber and add them to the fortress wall. Competition among the units grew keen; some men ran forward to within a half mile of the British assembly area to gather their material.

It was nearly three in the afternoon, and hot. Most of the men had emptied their canteens long ago. Daniel Wilkins mentioned this to Thompson, wondering aloud where and how they might find water at this point.

"There is no water to be had," Thompson replied thinly. "No water. But consider: As tired and thirsty as we are, those men in the fortress are a hundred times worse off.

"They have been twelve hours at least without food or water, and under cannon fire since early morning."

Looking up Breeds Hill toward the fort, tufts of earth could be seen flying in the air when a ball landed against or in front of its walls.

Thompson looked out toward the warships. It was almost hypnotic: From the side of one would come a flash of flame, then a belch of smoke, then, after what seemed a minute or more, a dull, booming sound. He shook his head to clear it, and bent to heft another load of brush.

Captain Crosby called out to Maxwell and Wilkins: "I have just returned from speaking with Colonel Stark." He drew closer and lowered his voice. "He is most concerned. He was informed by Colonel Prescott that he is losing men from the fort, and not from cannon fire. They are either sneaking away secretly or not returning after taking the wounded back to the mainland. So far he has lost more than a hundred of the eight hundred he had."

"Some of our men, too, have wandered away," said Wilkins. "But only a few. Private Small returned. But not private Brown."

Thompson felt a mixture of disappointment and frustration at the young private's defection—and relief that he had survived.

"Talk to them. Encourage them," Crosby was saying. "We will need every man. I've counted twenty-eight British troop barges ferrying men and cannon to the shore."

"Sir," said Thompson, meeting his commander's eyes as levelly as he could, "you have been forward with Colonel Stark. How many British do you think we have to fight?"

"Colonel Stark estimates at least fifteen hundred on shore now, with more coming. They will outman us two or three to one, but we have the benefit of high ground and what looks like a stone-and-log structure to protect our position."

They looked up toward the fortress in time to see Colonel Stark walking in a line parallel with its front wall and carrying what appeared to be a wooden stake wrapped in blue-and-white cloth. He seemed to be pacing out a distance. He stopped, at a point Thompson guessed to be forty yards in front of the wall, and hammered the stake into the ground with the butt of his pistol. Returning, he summoned Captain Crosby and a group of officers to his side.

Thompson and Daniel Wilkins, from where they stood, could not hear his words, which were these: "Your men will not fire until commanded. And in no instance before the British reach that mark"—he turned sideways to point to the stake. "We have little powder and shot to waste. You may as well know, there are but eight barrels of gunpowder available for the entire army in Massachusetts. Don't expect resupply."

Suddenly, strangely, the sound of cannon stopped. The silence was as stunning as the firing had been. In every company, the men paused in their labors to look about in surprise.

Up above at the fortress, Colonel Prescott could be seen walking along the line, talking to his men: "Shoot for the officers whenever possible," he told them, though this was not heard by his watchers below. "Those arrogant bastards. They think we will run on sight of their fine uniforms. We damn well will not!"

There came now the tapping of drums and the sound of fifes and, down the hillside, the movements of colorful squares of light infantry and grenadiers moving into place: formations, four deep, preparing for attack. It all moved slowly, so very slowly that it was agonizing to watch. The British, whatever else they intended, were obviously in no hurry to attack.

"It will be soon now," Prescott said. "Let me walk along your line with you, Colonel Stark, and do my best to embolden your men. If New Hampshire breaks, sir, the militia in the fortress will be surrounded with no chance of retreat. They will die like dogs."

"We will not break, Colonel Prescott," answered Stark, "be assured of it. Your men will live to fight another day. New Hampshire will not break."

18

JUNE 1775
AMHERST, THE ATHERTON FARM

JOSHUA HAD JUST EXTINGUISHED THE LANTERN and hung it on a peg protruding from a barn post. It was an hour past dawn, and there was more than enough light to see by. The sky was clear; the east-facing doors allowed the sun to flood the barn, effacing the early-morning shadows.

He had just turned from tending his horse when his ten-year-old daughter, Frances, burst into the barn, running, a pail of chicken feed in her hands. Her face was bright red. Crossing the threshold, she stumbled briefly, then caught herself on the doorpost, but not before the pail had smashed against the barn wall spilling the feed all over the floor. She seemed barely to notice: "Father! Oh, Father!" she cried.

"What is it, Frances? Calm yourself." Joshua approached her gently and laid a hand on her shoulder.

"Father, it's those men again. They're back, coming up the Post Road!"

"Are you quite certain?"

"Yes, yes!" Frances took her father by the hand, pulling him toward the door and the barnyard. Once in the doorway, she pointed, though there was no longer any need: "They are here!"

For a moment Joshua was speechless. Between ten and twenty armed militiamen were now streaming from the road, through the front gate and into the yard. They couldn't be the Amherst militia, Joshua thought, for he knew the militia to be with Captain Crosby, somewhere near Boston, under the command of Colonel Stark.

One of the men pointed in his direction and then spoke in a low voice to the man in front, whom Joshua now recognized as Daniel Campbell.

Campbell didn't acknowledge Joshua, or even his presence, but gestured instead toward the rear of the house. Half a dozen of the men broke off from the group, rounded the corner of the house, and headed for the rear yard.

Still holding Frances by the hand, Joshua walked closer to the men. "Mr. Campbell, what is the meaning of this?" he asked. "What do you want?"

Campbell turned, for the first time, to regard him. He was an imposing man, close to 250 pounds, little of it fat. He was known for his stamina as the leading land surveyor for the county—no one in Amherst could match his pace in the woods and swamps around town. Joshua wondered fleetingly if this might be some sort of land problem, but dismissed the thought immediately; armed men would hardly be needed for such a task.

Campbell, by now having dismounted, walked toward Joshua, two men flanking him. "We have received troubling information about you, Attorney Atherton," he said.

Joshua just looked at him, confused, silent, searching for some reply. Then came a scream from the direction of the house. It was Abigail. The kitchen door was thrown open behind her, and young Charles was running alongside in a panic, wailing at the top of his lungs.

"Joshua, what is this? There are men staring in my kitchen window! What is happening here?"

The sound of the scream and Charles's frightened tears seemed to take some of the bluster out of Campbell. He stepped back, a bit tentatively as Abigail approached—swift, uncowed, indignant, clearly expecting answers.

"Mister Campbell"—the contempt dripped from her voice. "Are these men with you? What is this about?" She held Charles by the shoulders, tight against her apron, and glared unblinking at Daniel Campbell, her face not a foot from his. Joshua almost laughed at the look on Campbell's face.

"Madam, Mistress Atherton, I was merely—"

"You were what exactly? Look what you have done to my son!" She scooped up Charles from the ground, to which he had fallen, his wails renewed at the sound of Campbell's voice.

Joshua knew his wife: Her anger would pass, it always did. But there was no sign yet of any ebbing. Campbell remained flustered, kicking the ground with the toes of his boots. Joshua squeezed his daughter's hand and waited for what would come next.

"Mrs. Atherton," Campbell began again. "Surely you know that Paul Dudley Sargent, Benjamin Kendrick, and I have been appointed Committee of Safety delegates to the County Congress."

Abigail remained rod-straight and unblinking.

"What has that got to do with your presence here, with these men surrounding my home, leering in my windows? What business have you here?"

Campbell was regaining his composure—it could be costly, in the presence of twenty men, to be seen as bending before the scorn of an aggrieved woman.

"Recently, the New Hampshire Assembly received a communication from the Continental Congress in Philadelphia, recommending that all persons considered possible dangers to the colonies be disarmed. Then, this past night, the Committee of Safety received a report that your husband is harboring a British officer, a spy, in your house."

Turning to face Joshua, he went on: "The Committee of Safety has cited you already as a possible enemy to the safety of New Hampshire as a result of your reported support of the king . . .

"And now this." His voice rose, attempting gravity. "It's most serious. Most serious indeed."

"Hogwash!" Joshua, emboldened, spat the words. "Absolute hogwash! You have known me for years—do you honestly think I would harbor a spy?"

"It makes no difference what I think," Campbell said icily, pompously, taking refuge in his duty and rank. "Orders have been given, and I will obey them. Your house must be searched. I ask that you cooperate, but if necessary we will accomplish our task without your leave."

"Joshua." Abigail's voice was low now, her anger drained or in hiding, he was not sure which. "Let them. It will bring an end to this."

Then she turned to Campbell.

"Mr. Campbell, you have your duty. Proceed with it then, but I warn you: Respect our property. You are looking for a man, not small items in cupboards, shelves, or drawers. I beseech you, remember that."

Campbell said nothing, only turned and walked back to his men. After a few moments' discussion, one group broke off to enter the house, while a second made for the barn and sheds. One unfortunate man was assigned the outhouse; young Frances, despite her terror, could not contain a giggle at this. Joshua smiled down at his daughter and squeezed her shoulder from behind.

The four of them—Abigail, Joshua, Frances, and Charles—stood by the barn with their arms around one another and waited until the soldiers had finished their job. Abigail stroked Charles's head. The sunny day seemed to have lost some of its luster. From behind came the sounds of stomping boots, furniture pieces scraping against floors, the cries and curses of men. Abigail's face was tense and white; Joshua could tell she had reached her limit: her home, her belongings, her very life, being violated—desecrated—by this ignorant mob of strangers. The pain he felt for her was as real as it was in vain.

After what seemed like hours, the men left the house and gathered around Campbell in the front yard. One of them was carrying Joshua's fowling piece. He started at the sight: the musket, once his father's, a quality piece that he prized. Abigail tightened the arm already around his waist. He felt himself relax.

Campbell, bearing the musket, came across the yard to them.

"Well, sir, are you satisfied?" Joshua asked, making no effort to conceal the edge in his voice. "You found nothing—no spy, no contraband, nothing except my fowling piece. Is that a danger to the community? What do you propose to do with it?"

"I'm sorry, Mr. Atherton, I must remove any and all weapons, no exceptions. I assure you it will be returned to you when this war is over."

Joshua opened his mouth, but once again felt Abigail's arm tighten around him. He was silent. Campbell, finished with his business, turned and walked back toward his men. Halfway there, he stopped in his tracks and turned once more:

"I'm sorry for your troubles, Mr. Atherton, Mrs. Atherton," he said, almost humbly. "I'm truly sorry. And I wish you well."

"I'm sorry as well, Daniel," Joshua answered softly. "For the troubles of us all."

19

BUNKER HILL

WITH THE CANNON BARRAGE FALLEN QUIET, the British closed ranks behind the sounds of fife and drum. As the British made their final preparations to attack, there came that interval that Thompson Maxwell, in his years as a soldier, had witnessed more times than he could say: that moment of inevitability, just prior to the first shots—the first deaths—when the tension is drawn as tightly as a bow. The only release for it, he knew well, was in false bravado: "Widows in England tonight!" "Redcoat bastards!" "Now taste the farmers' fire!"—all this from the New Hampshire line.

And from the British: "Cowards! Cowards, all of you!" "Come out, make yourselves seen, and feel the English blade!"

The men, Thompson knew, were approaching that stage of nerves that could deplete, then empty them—if it wasn't relieved soon by the opportunity to act. Waiting, he thought was among the worst hazards of war.

Then an odd, sudden silence fell over his line. He looked up from the powder horn he was filling. The faces of his men, though still staring down at the British formations, no longer showed fear or bravado, only plain, unalloyed shock. His eyes followed theirs down the slope to the shore: Two British companies were forming around a group of trees, with three bound soldiers being led forward, and ropes being draped across the largest tree limbs. Thompson stared in horror: so much random death to come today, and the British needed more bodies. He gazed into the distance so as not to view what came next.

There was a muffled cry beside him.

"Why did they do that?" It was Thomas Powell, the company's drummer boy, no more than fourteen years old. The terror was etched on his chalk-white face.

"They must have caught some deserters," Thompson said, as lightly as he could manage. "They do it as an example to the others." He rested his hand lightly on Thomas's shoulder. "It will be all right. It's normal to be afraid; we all are. Just keep by my side and we'll be back in Amherst before you know it."

The silence at last was broken. With the three doomed men still swaying from their tree limbs, the tapping of drums and the shrieking of fifes announced that the British, finally, would be mounting their attack. Still, it did not come swiftly. Each British unit began its march, in orderly blocks, four deep, up the beach. They would be attempting, from the looks of it, a frontal attack on the fortress, as well as a flanking maneuver along the Mystic River.

It was like watching a parade, Thompson thought, marveling anew at the contrast between the two armies: the British in their bright, spanking-clean uniforms of red, blue, and white, marching in precision, weapons gleaming in the sun; the Amherst militia in their dirty, homespun farm wear, no two dressed the same, bearing an array of muskets and fowling pieces of every type and caliber, many a quarter-century old. It would have been comical were not so many lives held in the balance.

Thompson's men seemed hypnotized by the pageantry. All eyes were glued to the approaching battalions. Quite abruptly, there came a movement to Thompson's right. He turned, just in time to see

Private Sawyer, the company clown, marching in a small circle, head high, shoulders squared, arms pumping in time to the music below.

"Sawyer, what the hell are you doing?"

"Oh, Lieutenant, sir, if they weren't trying to kill us, I'd think it was the finest parade I ever saw. I hope it won't be my last."

It had broken the spell—a ripple of laughter passed along the line. Thompson did his best to look stern as he gave the only order he could: "Sawyer, get back to the line or I'll send you down there to greet them."

Sawyer grinned, saluted, and took his place in the ranks.

The British were halfway up the beach now; the moment was nearing. Leaning his musket against the fence, Thompson rose to his feet and began his walk along the line, stopping at every second or third man, laying his hand briefly on a shoulder, calming the terror he knew was behind the dull eyes.

"Remember, your friends are beside you, and depending on you."

And always, he reminded: "The mark. Keep your eye on Colonel Stark's mark."

The men, most of them, acknowledged his presence—by a word, a nod, a small smile—but their eyes, for the most part, remained fixed on the advancing human wall.

The British light infantry moved along the beach in precise formation, muskets raised at 45-degree angles, each topped with a fourteen-inch blade. This would be, for a while yet, Thompson knew, a war of nerves. His own orders were not to fire until the British had reached Stark's flag—there could be no wasted ammunition—but the restraint this would require could very well be too much for his men. Thompson hoped not.

The British, he guessed, did not plan to fire, either. More likely they would rely on the bayonet to chase these untried farmers back home. It was a fearsome thought: an advancing unit, too many to bring down, then steel thrust cleanly into flesh. But it was the

View of the attack on Bunker Hill on June 17, 1775.
(Source: Bunker Hill Memorial Tablets, published by the City of Boston, 1889)

British way, it was what they were trained for. Firing practice was rare; when they fired at all, they did so as a unit: a massive, collective volley largely without aim.

Now, a hundred yards away, the officers standing to the rear of the British formations bellowed their orders. The infantry units swung around so that the full width of the four-deep formations faced the colonial ranks. Sunlight glittered on belt buckles, buttons, and the bright, cruel bayonet blades. They looked elegant, poised, utterly confident. In a brief moment of sickening doubt, Thompson wondered if the attacking force could somehow see through to the truth: the fear, the unreadiness, the lack of training, the overwhelming odds, and the illusionary barricade they had positioned themselves behind.

Just then Colonel Stark appeared along the line. "Aim for the buckle! Keep your shots low! Aim for the officers!"

To the Amherst farmers and shopkeepers, who in those moments surely felt exactly what they were, the British were a solid wall: slow, deadly, inexorable, a force unthinkable to resist.

"Stay low, on your knees!" It was Captain Crosby. "Wait, wait, until they cross the colonel's mark! I'll give the command!"

At that moment, all along the line, the British officers raised their swords, pointed to the fence, and barked their command for attack. In unison, the wall of red-coated soldiers dropped their muzzles to the attack position, bayonets horizontal, and surged ahead. A sergeant shouted over the din: "Forward, damn it! Forward! Give them the blade! Give them the blade!"

On command, the first light-infantry regiment surged toward the Amherst men. They neared Colonel Stark's fluttering flag—then were past it. Captain Crosby bellowed his command, followed an instant later by Thompson, Daniel Wilkins, and the other officers on the line: "Stand and fire!" "Fire! Fire! Fire!"

To a man, the line stood and fired. The thunder of a thousand guns was deafening. To miss was all but impossible, with the massed formations facing them at point-blank range. In the Amherst position alone, a hundred muskets cracked, smoke billowed, and for several seconds time stopped and everything was obscured.

Thompson heard Crosby a few meters to his right: "Don't look, reload and fire as fast as you can—fast, fast, fast!"

Thompson stood, poured powder into the barrel and spat a ball after it, then rammed it home. Cocking his musket, he primed the flash pan and knelt to fire again. He looked up, and prepared to take aim.

The smoke from the first volley was clearing; he was stunned by what he saw: The two front ranks of British were gone, eliminated. Great mounds of dead and dying lay stacked before him, their bright uniforms now dark with blood and powder burns. Some men groaned and writhed in pain; others lay still, a few heaped so close that it was impossible to distinguish one from the other.

The carnage had stunned the British as well. The rear ranks now stepped back, some soldiers tripping, then falling over one another. An officer toward the rear, standing, waved his sword in circles, urging his men forward. The last words were scarcely out of his mouth when his shout turned to a cough as a ball thudded into his stomach. Then, somehow, the British were coming ahead again, stepping on and over their comrades, prodded forward by sergeants and officers.

The colonists reloaded and fired. A second burst rent the air, then random shots as the militia reloaded at different speeds. A third volley smashed into the massed ranks of blue and redcoats.

Through the thick clouds of smoke, the regulars could be seen to hesitate, then to stop, and finally to turn and scatter, occasionally firing in retreat as they scampered like frenzied children down the hill. The officers shouted incitements: "Again to the fence! Move, move, damn you!" were all but useless.

Within minutes, except for the occasional sniper shot or cry from the wounded, the field was quiet. No drum or fife sounded; the officers' shouts had died down. The British, for now at least, were beaten—upward of two thirds of the leading attacking force in piles before the fence. Everywhere Thompson looked, up and down the line in front of the earthen fortress, the scene was the same.

A few of the British bayonets had reached their targets. There were some colonial dead and wounded, but relatively few. All in Thompson's company had survived uninjured, though in the next company over he saw two dead behind the fence. A dozen or so wounded men, two or three with deep chest wounds, were being helped or carried to the rear.

Stark and Prescott, Thompson knew, would be beginning to instill in the men just the right measure of confidence. It was critical that they not dwell too heavily on what was sure to be a second attack (though just as critical that they be ready for it) or on the carnage just beyond the fence. The commanders, as he watched, began their walk along the line: "Load and be ready. We can stop them again! This time continuous fire—they won't be expecting that!" The continuous-fire technique was a pairing of two men, one firing as the other loaded, preventing the enemy from having a lull during which to load themselves.

When Stark, now accompanied by Captain Crosby, reached the position of the Amherst militia in the line, Thompson stepped forward and approached: "Sir," he said, "with all due respect, perhaps we should strengthen the line in the locations where the British did not attack the first time. They'll be coming at us at different points, I believe, not wanting to trample the bodies of their dead."

Colonel Stark looked at Thompson—a studied, respectful look—then nodded. "You're probably right, Lieutenant," he said. "And thank you. I'll order that done."

For two hours, all was quiet. The British tended their wounded; the colonists readied themselves, cleaned weapons, ate whatever food they had. Then, looking down to the British staging area around mid-afternoon, Thompson saw what he had known would come in only a matter of time: the massing and movement of company after company assembling on the beach. Nothing, he thought, would be held in reserve this time. There was even a company of marines.

Again, as before, a solid line of soldiers, four deep, was advancing. How foolish, Thompson thought—it was 90 degrees in an afternoon sun, and the British were still in their heavy wool coats and full packs. The packs, he had heard, weighed a hundred pounds each.

On the colonial side, the men waited with patience, notwithstanding the occasional, against-orders stray shot. The British grenadiers were within one hundred yards now; General Howe himself could be seen climbing the hill behind the troops.

Howe was resolute: The second assault, more than a thousand men strong, would succeed. Weak spots in the colonial line would be used to full advantage; the fortress would be taken, the British regulars would pour through in an unstoppable wave. He was sure of it—there could not be more than five hundred patriots, untrained, and fighting with bird muskets to protect an earthen "fort." They had been lucky. They would not be lucky twice.

Along the rebel line the order was given for the men to crouch down so as not to let the British see that sections of the line that had escaped the first charge had been strengthened, and to let the British fire first, should that be their plan.

Then came the sounds of drums and fife and the start of the slow march forward. Line after line of grenadiers, light infantry, marines, finally the royal fusiliers—the force approached to within fifty yards of the fence. And now General Howe's order "Ready!"—echoed up and down the line.

The first line of men dropped to their knees and raised their muskets, as, simultaneously, the soldiers just behind stood and raised theirs. And now the command—"Fire!"—and a deafening cacophony of hundreds of muskets, as flame belched from the weapons and smoke descended everywhere. Instantly, the third and fourth British lines moved forward, changing positions with the first two. Then the second volley.

Even before the smoke cleared, the colonials were ready, as

Colonel Stark's command sounded along the line: "Rise and fire." A haze of smoke still partially obscured the British line, though nothing could hide it entirely: a solid, unbroken mass of men. Half the patriot guns thundered, then the second half as the first reloaded. They were firing almost blindly, which, thought Thompson, was perhaps just as well: Too much thinking at such a time could undo the faint of heart.

Turning to his right, then his left, he shouted his order: "Load and fire! Load and fire!" At the same time he caught glimpses, as the smoke began to clear, of casualties along his line. Not as many, though, as might have been expected. The British, once again, had fired high.

"Charge! The bayonet!"

General Howe's command rang across the field. The red, blue, and white line surged forward, stumbling over the dead and wounded.

As the British came closer, the rebel firing became selective: Every officer and sergeant in the Thirty-fifth Light Infantry and Tenth Grenadiers was killed or wounded; Lieutenant Page, of General Howe's own staff, had his ankle crushed by a shot. Lieutenant Jourdian and Captain Sherwin were killed in the exchange. Howe himself, remarkably, was unscathed, apparently shielded by his cluster of aides.

Again, as in the first assault, a few of the grenadiers reached the fence, but in numbers too small to do serious damage. In locations where the fence line was breached, the militia simply fell back a dozen steps and continued to fire at the British entangled in the fencing, stones, and straw.

To Thompson, all this seemed to take hours. In fact, less than ten minutes passed between General Howe's first order to fire and the moment the British halted, broke, and fell back. As before, they fled to the staging area, firing sporadically in retreat.

Cheering broke out along the militia line as fear, in the space of seconds, was replaced by bravado: "What do you think of us now?" "Come back, we'll give you more!"

But it died away quickly as the smoke cleared further and the men took in the full scene: the bodies of their fallen comrades—there were more this time—as well as the appalling multitude of British dead near the fence. Indeed, there was scarcely an area of dirt or grass not covered by dead or broken bodies.

Daniel Wilkins came over to Thompson: "We seem to have been spared once again," he said, "but they will be back."

"Yes," said Thompson, for these were the very thoughts he had, "and with a fury beyond anything we have seen. They have never known defeat such as this. They will not leave it here."

With the tension lifted for the moment, Thompson could feel his own exhaustion and the sting of smoke and powder in his eyes. His mouth was dry and tasted bitter. Looking at Wilkins, he almost laughed at the sight of the man's face—stained gray, with some of his beard and hair singed from musket fire. He himself must look no better, he thought.

Captain Crosby came running up to the two men: "Prescott's aide has informed me that the right flank suffered heavy losses before the British fell back. Your New Hampshire militia must now be moved nearer the fort to replace the losses there. There are fewer than three hundred men within."

"Surely, sir," answered Wilkins, "there couldn't have been so many casualties as that. There were eight hundred men before."

"I'm afraid casualties are the lesser problem now. The men appear to believe their luck is wearing thin, that the British will mount a successful charge next time. Many are drifting away; others, who helped the wounded to safety in the rear, are not returning."

Crosby departed. Thompson walked along the line of Amherst men, offering encouragement and taking a mental inventory of each soldier's supplies. Some were without musket balls, others out of powder. The powder, he knew, could be replenished from the British dead and wounded. He dispatched a squad for that purpose. Lead balls, though, were another matter: While standardization was the rule among the British, the balls of the colonial militia were of many sizes—each one fitted to the musket of its owner. Thompson gave his foraging squad the only order he could: to collect the largest balls they could from the British dead and wounded, then pass them out to the men, who would hammer them down to fit. On average, he calculated, the Amherst company had fewer than four balls left per man.

They waited. Many, Thompson suspected, were no doubt anxious to run, but none did, or none that he saw. Not a man among them, he imagined, was willing to be the first to desert his friends. But how much longer could they hold? Hunger and thirst were pervasive; they had had nothing to eat since morning, and their canteens were surely long dry.

"Consider the men in the fort," Daniel Wilkins exhorted some of the men as he made his way along the line. "They have had nothing to eat and little to drink since last evening. If they can manage, then so can we."

Crawling low from one end of the fence to the other, Thompson took a rough count of the British casualties. The entire field, from the Mystic River beach to near the fort, was covered with bodies, sometimes lying two and three thick. Returning, he located Captain Crosby. "There must be five hundred dead, sir, maybe more," he said.

"I didn't think we could do it, but we did," Crosby answered, then lowered his voice and turned to face Thompson; there were men near enough to hear: "But can we hold one more time, Lieutenant? Can we bring these men to believe in themselves?

"That, sir," replied Thompson—a bit grimly, Crosby thought— "will be the task."

The rebels' euphoria was short-lived.

The barges ferrying British wounded from Charlestown to Boston were returning with reinforcements, regiments of Royal Marines and light infantry. Accompanying them off the boats was Gen. John Clinton, a new arrival to the scene.

General Prescott, from his lookout at the top of the fortress, recognized him instantly.

"There! There!" he shouted excitedly, gathering two marksmen around him, pointing at Clinton disembarking from the ferry: "The man in the hat—he's the general! Fire, you men! Fire!"

The two men fired, but the distance was too great for accuracy. The closest ball struck Clinton's aide in the neck. He slumped to the ground.

Undeterred by this, or, apparently, by the sight of the wounded massed on the beach, Clinton strode among the reinforcements. Short, stocky, and exuberant, he walked and talked with all the enthusiasm of a new recruit, stopping often to chat with company officers or study the fortress from below. His vigor seemed to energize the men.

With the forces he had left, General Howe and his few surviving officers attempted—half successfully—to cajole, threaten, and beat the weary and defeated men into new formations: mixed units of ten to fifty survivors each. It was the British now who wore the mismatched uniforms, barely distinguishable under their cover of blood and grime.

Thompson, looking down the hill at the assembling force, could see soldiers to his rear on Bunker Hill, though none yet seemed to be moving ahead. So far, he thought, the Amherst militia had been fortunate: Of the seventy men at the fence, only John Cole had fallen, shot through the head with a musket ball. Still, too many men were disappearing, slipping off unnoticed, or remaining behind the lines with wounded friends. Company strength was down to fifty men, with powder and shot for only a few volleys each. Thompson shook his head. It would never be enough.

Turning, he saw Colonel Stark, with Captain Crosby, walking down the line once again: "Just stop them one more time," Stark said encouragingly, to man after man, sounding for all the world as if he had no doubt it could be done. Thompson admired his faith—

or leadership. As they drew nearer, Captain Crosby motioned him over. "I wish I could offer you reinforcements. I just can't." He said it flatly. Thompson only nodded.

"The fortress is in worse condition than here," said Stark. "Fewer than four hundred men, and most without any means to fight. They will be supplied first, if anyone is."

Gesturing behind him, toward Bunker Hill, he continued: "Colonel Ward refuses to send his men forward. He is insisting the British will ferry troops around him for a landing at Charlestown Neck. That's nonsense, of course, but he won't budge."

All Thompson could do was nod. His mouth felt so dry he wasn't sure he could speak.

"Ward is stupid," Stark fairly bellowed. "Stupid or a coward, and I will give him the benefit of the doubt. Do your best here." With those last words, he turned abruptly and continued along the line.

It would be soon, Thompson thought, watching as the British in the assembly area below began removing their packs and heavy coats and flinging them to the ground.

"They're getting ready!" Crosby said.

Down the slope, past the mounds of still bodies beginning to stink in the 90-degree heat, rank after rank of blue and red uniforms could be seen beginning to move.

"At least they must be as hot and tired as we are," the man next to Thompson said, pointing to the west side of the peninsula. He was quiet for a second, then added, "Those fresh reinforcements—it looks as though they're climbing to attack the fortress, not us."

It was the collection of mismatched uniforms that climbed the slope towards the fence line, but not strung out along the entire line. This time they were massed along the western side of the slope, closer to the fortress than to the Mystic River shore.

"Ready, be ready! Let them get close! We have no powder to waste!"

The men of the New Hampshire militia waited. Some seeing the four-deep wall of British regulars approaching to within the firing location retreated; others remained at their post even though it was a certainty that the thin defensive line, now with gaps of three to four feet between men, could not hold.

Suddenly, from behind the British formation, a command was given and the attackers shifted to the west to join the fresh troops about to attack the fort. The entire British force headed in a straight line for the fort. But nothing like before: no drums or fifes this time, and the famed British order was gone. The advancing men were screaming, swearing, firing off their muskets as they came, an angry mob, Thompson thought, intent only on revenge. Never before had he heard of a British regiment attacking in such a way.

To the defenders in the fort, it was no use. The British forces, fifteen hundred strong, took the fort. General Prescott and most of his four hundred men withdrew. Seeing that the fort could not hold, Captain Crosby and other New Hampshire militia officers ordered the fence line abandoned. The New Hampshire militia fell back, to develop a defensive line to support the withdrawing Americans as they crossed Charlestown Neck. The rest of Prescott's men, abandoned in the fort and without powder or other weapons, could only use their muskets as clubs. They were slaughtered in minutes, bayoneted to death where they stood by a furious adversary, bent on revenge for the carnage they were subjected to, and that by cowardly rebels.

The British, exhausted and battle-weary, did not give chase to the retreating colonial forces. They had wanted only the fortress. And revenge.

The rebels, on their initial return to Cambridge, were plunged into the deepest sort of gloom as they viewed their loss of the fortress, in what came to be known as the Battle of Bunker Hill, as a crushing, ignominious defeat.

In time, though, as information was received from Boston—and later from London it became clear that Bunker Hill, for the colonial army, had been a victory of the first order. There were 411 colonial casualties as against 1,200 for the British, including 92 of the estimated 250 officers who had taken part, and the resultant replacement of Gov. Gen. Thomas Gage by Gen. William Howe.

Among the British dead was Maj. John Pitcarin, the officer credited with holding together the British forces in their earlier retreat from Concord. He was struck by one of the last shots from the fortress before it was overpowered by his men.

20

AUGUST 1776
AMHERST, THE ATHERTON FARM

IT WAS MID-AFTERNOON, the hottest hour of one of the hottest days of the year—the worst possible time, thought Joshua, to be hoeing his garden. But it was work that had to be done.

Drenched in sweat, he paused for a second, leaning on his hoe in the shade of a passing cloud. His back ached mightily, and still two hours, work to do. Weeding was no joy, he thought, even in cooler weather. But lately there had been little else to occupy his time. And the income from the garden's produce was the primary source of the family's livelihood.

Smiling to himself, still leaning on his hoe, he remembered that his father had wanted him to be a farmer. But his health had been poor—he lacked the energy and stamina necessary for the long days in the fields—and he had chosen the law instead. And here he was a farmer, perhaps the only one in the colonies with a degree from Harvard and an attorney's certificate on his wall. A certificate, yes, but no law practice to accompany it. His attorney's grant as well as his royal commission as register of probate and justice of the peace were taken from him by the new government.

The year since the battle of Bunker Hill had not been kind to

Joshua Atherton, nor to his family. At first it had been only a matter of the shunning; then it progressed to sneers in the street, verbal insults, vandalism, finally violence. Not a month went by without some physical act against his property, almost always at night: rocks thrown against the house, musket shots in the air, the occasional animal carcass over the front fence. And as the months passed and General Washington's war grew longer and more costly, the attacks became more frequent, more personal.

Except for church, the Atherton family no longer attended public meetings. The Hillsborough County meeting, in late spring, had been the last. A mitigated disaster: Some inopportune remarks on his part about the advisability of negotiations with the king, countered by a string of vitriol, resulted in insults, rotten eggs, the degradation of being spat on, finally physically eviction.

Then, only two nights after the county meeting, the utter humiliation: a ten-man "escort" to Jones Tavern to face the Committee of Safety, there subjected to another demand that he sign the Association Test Paper. That cursed document, he thought.

The Continental Congress in Philadelphia demanded all men above the age of twenty-one years to sign, except slaves and the insane, as if the mere signing an oath of allegiance to the new government would prove one's loyalty.

This time, though, it had not been Matthew Patten doing the talking, but, rather, Daniel Campbell, as boorish a figure as Joshua had ever known. Even today, months later, he still woke up sweating from dream reprisals of the scene:

"You, Joshua Atherton, are a danger to the safety of America!" Campbell had thrust his outstretched finger across the tavern table and into Joshua's chest. At the table were at least fifteen men, all pushing in for the sport. Joshua had felt his face redden; he was near to losing control. Before he could check himself, he leapt to his feet, followed instantly by Campbell. Now the two of them were face to face, separated only by the narrow table.

"You would strike me, Atherton? Strike me? Here, in the presence of these men? Is it not enough that you have been stripped of your post as registrar, that you can no longer practice law? Do you wish now to assault a member of the Committee of Safety and to spend the balance of the war in a cell?"

Campbell turned to face the assembled men, who by now could have been called a mob: "Is any more proof needed, gentlemen, that this man is a danger to America, a danger to the patriot cause?"

Joshua, although never a violent man, had been pushed past tolerance. He was on the verge of leaping across the table, of seizing Daniel Campbell by the neck, when Robert Means, the loyal, long-suffering Robert Means, stood up between the two. Staring directly into Campbell's eyes, he spoke softly, yet there was no mistaking the threat:

"Mr. Campbell," he said, "let us not sink to the levels that we both know are occurring elsewhere. New Hampshire is a small colony; we lived together peacefully before our revolution, and I pray we will do so again, as citizens of a free country. Now, as one member of the Committee of Safety to another, I ask that you state your accusations against Mr. Atherton calmly, then allow him to respond."

With that, he placed a hand firmly on Daniel Campbell's arm and eased him back down into his chair. The men around the table, disappointed, mumbled into their mugs of cider and rum. Campbell, perhaps sensing he would be no match for Joshua with Means as an ally, chose to defer: "No, Robert," he said, in a manner that showed that he had lost all taste for the business of the evening. "I think it best if you continue in my place."

Means, pulling some papers from his saddlebag, placed them on the table, then turned to Joshua. His voice was gentle but firm. "Joshua," he said, "following your remarks at the county meeting two nights past, our committee was asked to give you one final opportunity to sign the Association Test Paper. So far, only four men in Amherst—including yourself—have failed to sign. Will you join us? I beseech you, as your friend and as a citizen of New Hampshire."

For several moments, the room was quiet. Then Daniel Campbell, unable to contain himself a second longer, burst in: "Dammit, Atherton! I don't know why we continue to cater to you. No one else has been requested a second time! Sign the paper, Atherton! Get on with it, or consider yourself a threat to the safety of New Hampshire and accept the consequences. There is no other way!"

Joshua regarded Campbell quizzically, then put forth his hands, palms down, in a gesture that asked for quiet. He spoke clearly, in a voice that all in the room could hear, but looked only at the two men.

"I'm sorry, sir, that I lost my temper. You, Mr. Means, and you, Mr. Campbell, and all these men here, you are just performing the task ordered of you by our new state government."

"Why, for God's sake, why?" It was Means who spoke, pleading. "Sign the document. The provisions are not onerous; let me again read them."

After some fumbling, he placed his half-glasses on his face and read: " 'We the subscribers, do hereby solemnly engage and promise that we will do the utmost of our power, at the risk of our lives and fortunes, with arms oppose the hostile proceedings of the fleets and armies, against the United American Colonies.'

"How can you find this so repugnant?"

Turning to his friend, Joshua replied softly. All fight seemed to have gone out of him. "I do not find it repugnant, Robert. I simply cannot sign it. Even at this late date, I cannot condone violence to solve this dispute."

Robert Means could only shake his head in disappointment. "Joshua, I beseech you. If only for your family, you—."

Joshua interrupted him. "No. You must understand. It's for the future of my family that I refuse."

His voice increased in volume. Everyone around the table was riveted.

"Our New Hampshire Constitution," he went on, "adopted last January—the first such constitution in America—speaks of freedom and liberty. Your test paper speaks of an armed confrontation. I believe in the force of law, of reason, not of muskets. I cannot in good conscience sign."

The tavern was quiet; the men around the table were listening. Joshua, thinking this might be his last opportunity, rose to his feet and continued: "The greatest harm we can accomplish is to trade one tyrant for another, King George for one of our own making. The liberty and freedom of which we speak embrace more than acts; they embrace the freedom to think and speak our mind."

Paul Dudley Sargent started to rise. Robert Means leaned over, placed a hand on his shoulder, and spoke quietly to him. Sargent settled back down. Means nodded to Joshua. "Go on," he said.

"New Hampshire's constitution, adopted in January, established the people's government—two branches, the House of Representatives and the Council—a government specifically charged by the constitution to preserve the peace and good order of New Hampshire. The constitution further states, Mr. Campbell, that the government is to preserve the security of the lives and the property of the inhabitants.

"These are the rights I feel you are violating with these inquisitions and your 'association test' document."

Daniel Campbell jumped up from his chair.

"Hogwash! You have enhanced the document beyond its purpose! Do you not agree, Mr. Means?"

Robert Means spoke slowly, almost ceremonially: "No, sir, I do not agree. I have read the constitution, and it reflects Attorney Atherton's view. I do not agree with him that negotiation with Britain is still possible considering the war at hand, but I do agree that we must preserve our personal freedoms as Attorney Atherton states. If we neglect our duty to do so, and maintain our loyalty to the constitution in the same breath—we are guilty of hypocrisy, nothing less."

"Mr. Campbell," said Joshua, "I accept your Committee of Safety as the executive branch of the New Hampshire government, and that you have been charged to ferret out those who are considered a danger to the liberty of the community. But I have been cruelly and unfairly accused of being such an enemy, and I would make two requests of you."

Campbell, attempting, belatedly, to take charge of the meeting once again, and chagrined by Robert Means's failure to support him, stood to face Joshua. He spoke in the same thick bluster with which he had begun.

"Attorney Atherton," he said, "you are in no position to make demands. It is we who are here to demand of you."

"Mr. Campbell," Means said, "there will be no solution here today. You can see that Attorney Atherton is resolute in his position. Why not allow him his two requests?"

Campbell said nothing, only looked down at the table and shook his head. Joshua took this as assent: "Thank you, Robert. You are very kind. You have always been kind.

"First, I would request a hearing, a fair judicial tribunal, as is my right. The Committee of Safety is a branch of the legislature. Legislatures make laws; but it is the court that interprets laws. So then, let it be a jury of my peers who decide if I am a danger to the safety of New Hampshire."

Campbell's answer was quick in coming: "Attorney Atherton, the same has been requested by other Tories before you. The decision has always been the same, that the power, the total power to judge, shall remain with the Committee of Safety, not the judges. What is your second request?"

"My second request, yes." Joshua looked out over the cluster of men. Spying Captain Hildreth, the tavern proprietor, in the rear of the room, he addressed him across the heads of the others: "Captain Hildreth, this meeting has been heated and confrontational, but I consider all, though I disagree with them, to be fellow citizens, some even friends. To show that I bear no ill will, I request that these gentlemen be given the hospitality of your tavern. And at my expense."

There was a long silence. Embarrassed laughter, then controlled bedlam erupted as the men rose from their places and pushed toward the small bar. Daniel Campbell, unnoticed by anyone, ground his fists against the underside of the table. He misread Joshua's generosity, thinking that Atherton was attempting to show he was too clever for them all.

Glaring at him, seething quietly, he made a silent vow: He would do whatever was necessary, pay whatever price to see Joshua Atherton molder, for as long as possible, with his Tory cronies in the safety of the county jail.

All that was months ago and Joshua had heard nothing since, except that Daniel Campbell was petitioning all who would listen to declare him a Tory spy. Joshua was resigned to the fact that he had made a permanent enemy of him. And of Judge Claggett, for that matter, and most of the rest of the Committee of Safety, and no doubt others—it was hard to know, at times like these, who might be counted as a friend.

But here, in the August heat, with his back aching and two hours worth of hoeing still to do, the chaos of war and politics seemed remote, of another world.

His solitude was broken as he heard his name called, warmly, from the road. Turning, he saw Robert Means approaching across his field, carefully stepping over every planted row.

Joshua waved and started toward him, though he knew this could not be good. Robert was a close friend, but wary, even so, of being seen with Joshua; most of their visits over the past year had been at night, at one or the other's home. To have come here like this, at midday. . . . Joshua doubted this visit would bring good news.

"Joshua, Joshua, forgive the interruption. You looked as if you were asleep leaning on your hoe."

"No reason to apologize, Robert. It is wonderful to see you."

"I couldn't wait until night to come. The county Committee of Safety has received instructions. Not good, I'm sorry to say."

Joshua shook his head and gripped his friend's hand heartily.

"No matter. It's always good to see you, old friend. Give me the worst of it."

"I petitioned the House and Council, as you requested. The Provincial Committee of Safety in Exeter was called to discuss your request for a trial by your peers. The meeting was going well until Judge Claggett arrived.

"Claggett reminded them what they surely knew already but had seemed almost prepared, in your case, to forget—that the same request has been made by others and refused. Then there was his warning that if we tried every accused Tory, it would clog the courts for years.

"In the end, there was almost no support for your position. It was decided that the power to arrest and imprison Tories had been granted to the various Committees of Safety, and would remain with them . . . .

"I'm sorry, Joshua."

For a moment Joshua remained leaning against his hoe, saying nothing. Then he gave a long sigh and smiled wistfully at his friend. "I suspect, then, that it is only a matter of time."

"Yes," replied Robert, "but I doubt anything will happen soon. You still have the respect of most in Amherst; others think you harmless. I wish I could do more. But it is past me now."

"Thank you, Robert. Please, if you will, say nothing to your wife. Nor to Abigail."

"Of course not, Joshua."

The two men walked across the field to the Post Road, where they locked hands, hugged briefly, then parted.

21

DECEMBER 1776, AMHERST

As it turned out, Joshua was right: The failure of General Washington's army through the fall and winter of 1776-1777 made it more obvious by the week that the war could not be won.

The only bright spot was the evacuation of Boston by General Howe in March, and even this was more a function of British strategy than of colonial might. And from March on, as though to squash any hopes that might have arisen, the colonial army suffered an almost unbroken string of increasingly stinging defeats.

The first was the battle of Brooklyn Heights, where, under the command of New Hampshire's Gen. John Sullivan (who had earned short-lived fame for his "victory" against the virtually undefended Fort William and Mary in December 1774), 970 colonial soldiers were killed or wounded, and another 1,000—including Sullivan—taken prisoner by the British. After that came the battle of Fort Washington on the Hudson River north of New York, where General Howe, following a brilliant flanking maneuver, forced the surrender of 3,000 colonial troops—reducing the rebel army by fully one fourth of its men.

Meanwhile, back in Amherst, no one provided Joshua with any of this news. He was an outcast, a pariah, a danger to the safety of the colonies. On Sundays at church, or on his daily walks, he was treated civilly but icily; no one lingered in conversation with such a man—the Committee of Safety, it was said, had eyes on every corner, at every meeting of men.

Joshua's only sources of news were the *New Hampshire Gazette* out of Portsmouth, the *Exeter Morning Chronicle,* and the occasional copy of a Boston paper supplied by Robert Means. It mattered little that many of these journals were weeks old, or older. He read them hungrily, from cover to cover, there being little else, outside of writing letters, to fill his winter days. He missed the camaraderie of other lawyers, the prestige he had enjoyed as registrar of probate for the county, though he would admit so to no one, not even his wife.

Abigail saw the state he was in and worried for him, never more so than on the days he spent writing his letters: to former friends and acquaintances, many of them now active in the Revolutionary government, who only rarely, she noticed, sent replies.

One late afternoon, following a full day watching him as he wrote at his secretary in the parlor, she could contain herself no longer: "That is the third letter you have sent to Josiah Bartlett in Philadelphia," she said. "He has replied to neither of the first two. Why do you continue to have such faith in that friendship? You have not seen him in more than two years."

"He is a man of importance, Abigail, a member of our Continental Congress. He could be influential in securing peace."

"Peace perhaps. But when you speak of peace, you mean it only on the terms *you* envision. Josiah Bartlett and the others, if they saw things as you do, Joshua, they would not be part of our government. They would have written you back, yet they have not.

"Even in Amherst, our own neighbors—Joshua, they turn from you in the street. Does that not tell you all you need to know?"

With a low sigh, she turned her back and took a step to go, knowing she had hurt him, fully expecting that there might now be silence between them for days. It was like that with her husband lately: When wounded or angry, he would retreat to some place she could not reach or comprehend, some place inside himself.

Instead, before she could take a second step, his arms were around her waist. "It will be all right," he said. "You'll see. They are my friends. They will not betray me." He spoke sadly and with effort, as though needing badly to believe his own words.

But Abigail was frightened. She knew better than to believe him. She had seen it herself, two days before, on the street in Amherst, the final, unarguable proof that her husband was either a dreamer or a fool.

She had been on her way from the meetinghouse after speaking with Mr. Wilkins when, from somewhere behind her, came the sounds of a wagon and the clanking of metal. She turned to witness a small band of armed militia escorting a dozen or so prisoners, who were shuffling along in chains attached to the back of a cart. The prisoners' clothes were dirty and in tatters; some of the men seemed barely able to walk.

She continued to stare, riveted, speechless, feeling the crowd around her slowly growing as she watched. At some point she realized the truth: that these men were not common criminals. Their clothing was in shreds, but of quality—some wore riding boots, others full coats and vests. As she continued to gape, a woman nearby answered the question she might not have dared ask:

"They are Tories from New York. The Committees of Safety from their towns have sent them here to be confined in our jail for the duration of the war."

"But why here?" Abigail asked, the seeds of terror taking root in her stomach and chest. "Why New Hampshire? Why Amherst?"

"Their local committees thought it would be safer, away from the British who are garrisoned in New York."

It was Daniel Campbell's wife, Abigail realized. As the woman spoke, she smiled thinly and looked straight at Abigail, her lips barely parting to allow the words to escape. "And we were offered a fee for the service, Mrs. Atherton."

Abigail had said nothing, at the time, to Joshua. But the fear grew larger, and she knew she would not be able to keep silent for long.

The next day, returning home from his daily walk to Robert Means's store, her husband had burst into the house as though the war itself had just been won. "Abigail! Abigail! Hilarious news!" Joshua grasped her by the arm, pulling her toward him, then yanked a sheet of paper from his coat.

"Last Thursday, fourteen New York Tories arrived here. They had them in chains, to be imprisoned in our jail for the term of the war!"

"I know, Joshua. I saw them arrive. It was a pathetic sight."

"A pathetic sight they may have been, but they weren't pathetic the next night!"

"Whatever do you mean?"

"They broke jail and escaped. The Committee of Safety is demanding that the militia go in pursuit!" Joshua began laughing.

"But it's even better than that." He was now waving the paper before her as though it were a flag.

"One of the men, a John Hitchcock, was reportedly a poet. He left this message for the esteemed Daniel Campbell—I copied it from Robert's copy. Listen to this, Abigail! Just listen to this!"

With a final guffaw and an exaggerated flourish, Joshua began reading:

> "Come all ye people, hear the rout,
> The jail is broke, the pris'ner' 're out
> Resolving to be free;
> So mount your horses, load your guns,
> And see you catch them every one,
> And bring them back to me.
>
> "I heard a man from Wilson say,
> That just about break of day,
> As he to market came,
> To sell his butter and his cheese,
> He spied some Tories he believed,
> Straightway a marching home.

"Pull off for blood and raise the town,
Be careful to waylay the ground
Before they you pass by;
Watch every hollow, plain and ridge
And set a guard at every bridge,
And catch them nappingly.

"For all the people know it round,
That I'm COMMITTEE for our town
And these men be lost,
I'll venture fifty pounds to one,
That if Congress hear they're gone,
That I shall lose my post."

Joshua was laughing so hard that his face was red; he was having trouble catching his breath. It was only as he reached for a handkerchief and brought it to his eyes that he noticed Abigail, who looked at him grimly, almost menacingly. It was a look he had not seen before.

"Don't see the humor? Campbell, his committee, and the jailer are livid. They're the laughingstock of Amherst, possibly of all New Hampshire once the news has spread."

Abigail's voice was ice: "No, I don't see the humor at all. Not for the Atherton family. Oh, the Whigs might have a laugh, they have nothing to fear from the Committee of Safety. But Tories, Loyalists, men such as yourself . . . . It is you, Joshua—we, us—who will bear the brunt of Campbell's embarrassment. How can you be so blind?"

The gaiety drained from Joshua. He put both arms around his wife's shoulders and drew her to him. "I'm sorry," he said. "Of course. Of course, you're right."

But she was limp in his arms, her head turned sideways, her eyes staring blankly, as though what they saw was too painful to bear.

In Philadelphia the Continental Congress took a reactionary response to its dissatisfaction with the performance of General Washington and his insistent demands for additional soldiers and supplies. Even worse than Washington losing battle after battle, the personal safety of Congress was at stake. General Howe had control of most of the land around Philadelphia; at times the city was defenseless. The solution: Make the Loyalists, many still safely harbored and prospering in the provinces, pay. By imprisoning or ejecting them, all possible spies would be eliminated, and their property could be sold to fund the war. A most effective solution. A recommendation was promptly sent to the thirteen provincial assemblies and the Committees of Safety: Arrest or eject all persons regarded to be dangerous to the liberties of America.

22

SPRING 1777
EXETER, NEW HAMPSHIRE

ABIGAIL HAD BEEN RIGHT. For the Tories of New Hampshire, and for the Atherton family in particular, there had been little cause for merriment once winter turned to spring.

In 1776, when the New Hampshire House of Representatives was not in session, the full power of the New Hampshire government was entrusted to the Committee of Safety. The authority to comply with the Philadelphia recommendation—or not—lay in the hands of one Meshech Weare, president of the council, chief of the New Hampshire courts, and head of the state Committee of Safety. With the legislature in adjournment for the season, Weare had ordered that the Philadelphia recommendation, with his approval and signature added, be printed and distributed to the committees in every county and town in the colony. In Amherst, the fourteen shackled Tories Abigail had witnessed, the ones whose escape Joshua had later found so hilarious, had been the early casualties of the Continental Congress's decree. Now, it seemed, it would be New Hampshire's turn to suffer the epidemic of mob mentality in the name of freedom.

Still, the Athertons had faith in the fairness of the Amherst citizens, but less than two weeks later it had been Joshua's turn.

The pot of breakfast porridge had just being hung on the fire-place crane when six armed men broke through the door. The unexpected loud snap of the door latch startled Abigail; she turned toward the front hall, dropping the pot and its liquid contents into the fire. "Joshua," she screamed. Before he could fully rise from his chair, though, two men grabbed him by his arms and pulled him to his feet. The leader barked "Quiet" and announced, "We have been ordered by the Committee of Safety to secure Squire Atherton, then bring him to the meetinghouse.

Dragged from his house, coatless, in the presence of his wife and terrified children, he was forcibly marched by two armed men through the wet spring snow and crusted ice to the meetinghouse, where he was tried, convicted, and ordered imprisoned, all in less than an hour.

"You have had your trial!" Daniel Campbell screamed at him from where he sat, at one end of a long table—Joshua sat alone at the other—with the other members of the Amherst Committee of Safety. "And a fair one it was, at that!"

Joshua had requested, respectfully, and only once, that he be permitted to confront his accusers. His petition, as he expected, was denied. He rose to protest, again respectfully, and was barely on his feet when he felt strong hands on his shoulders pushing him back down. Looking up, he saw it was Daniel Green, a young farmer who'd developed a mean streak since his betrothed had declined to marry him due to the ugly musket-ball wound to his face.

"Squire Atherton"—it was John Bradford now, another member of the committee, who addressed Joshua in a conciliatory tone, "Recommendations for this tribunal and your imprisonment have come from Philadelphia and Exeter. Your correspondence is in our hands. We have reviewed the letters; they speak for you. No witnesses are necessary, nothing need be said on your behalf. Had you signed the loyalty oath, of course, it might be easier to be sympathetic to your plight. But your letters, and your refusal, took this matter from our hands."

With Green's strong hands still pressing on his shoulders, Joshua said nothing, only nodded. It all seemed perfunctory now.

Then came the final piece of business: the offer of "free passage for you and your family to leave New Hampshire with the understanding that your home, and all personal property you leave behind, will then belong to the New Hampshire."

Joshua had looked straight at Daniel Campbell. "No," he said quietly. "Amherst is my home. My loyalties are here, irrespective of what your committee believes."

That had been the end of it. "Escort the prisoner to a wagon," Daniel Campbell had bellowed. Joshua, with Daniel Green, his silent, sullen armed escort, was loaded into a wagon like a sack of grain and tethered to the floor by a chain. As the wagon jerked forward, throwing him against the wooden side, he looked back to the small throng of citizens that had gathered in front of the meetinghouse. He saw Abigail, weeping and being held by Mary Means. Then shivering in the cold and sleet, bounced and jolted by every rock and rut on the road, he was taken to Exeter and jail.

It had been his home now for nearly a week: a tiny, square patch of dirt floor inside a room perhaps twenty feet to a side that was also home to another dozen or so fetid, stinking men. There was a row of straw against one wall and a single rough wooden bench, though neither was used by the cell's inhabitants, who sat or lay, rarely moving and mostly silent, around the perimeter wall. In the six days he had been here, Joshua had spoken at length with only one of his fellow prisoners, a Rev. Frederick Pitts of Albany, New York. It was Pitts who had been kind enough to help him to adjust to his surroundings after three days of lying curled in a ball, to straighten his badly cramped legs. "Thank you," Joshua had said weakly, and collapsed back against the wall. "That's all right," Pitts had answered. "The first week is always the worst."

On the fourth morning he had been awakened by a boot in his side and the sound of his muttered name.

"Mister Atherton, Mister Atherton, the superintendent wishes to see you."

Two men then took him up by the arms and half led, half dragged him to a small room somewhere nearby. Try as he did, he could not manage to straighten his legs. Still numb from the cold, blinded by the sudden light, and dazed from the rudeness of his awakening, it took him fully a minute to feel the warmth of the fire by his feet.

"Let him rest in that chair, over there," came a voice from the end of a table he seemed to be sitting near. He squinted and looked up, barely making out the shape of a man who, as Joshua's eyes grew accustomed to the light, came gradually into focus around a short red beard and weathered skin.

"You must excuse me, I have the advantage on you—your arrest papers. Otherwise I would not have known you. I am Thomas Gilman. We met when you assisted my employer in court here two years ago. Thanks to you, I kept my post. Later I received this appointment."

"Yes, I remember," Joshua replied, studying the man. "Please forgive my memory. You have prospered, it seems."

Turning to one of the guards, Gilman directed that a cup of tea be brought. After it had arrived and Joshua had taken his first taste, Gilman spoke again: "You were brought here for two reasons," he said, "First, to make certain the papers are in order; and second, so that I might talk to you, advise you how to survive this ordeal."

Gilman then went on to describe conditions at the prison: how the building housed four times the number it should, the high incidence of sickness and death—especially among the Tories, as common criminals were of a "hardier stock"—the necessity for the prisoners to pay for their own food and clothing, the various rules that governed daily life.

"I will keep you in the cell with the other Tories, not with the criminals; they would cut your throat for those fine boots alone. But I can do only so much, you understand."

Joshua nodded, recalling the details of how he had helped Mr. Gilman's employer two years before, and saved Gilman from losing his post.

The paperwork completed, Joshua was escorted back to his cell, feeling a bit better for the half hour of warmth, the kind words, the cup of tea. The thick thud of the cell door closing behind him seemed an insult, the damp cold and smell of body wastes the more over-powering in contrast to the kindness and comfort he had briefly enjoyed.

Frederick Pitts raised his head when Joshua entered.

"So, you met with Mr. Gilman, eh? And he treated you civilly? And now, of all things, you feel worse?"

Joshua smiled bitterly, nodded, and slumped to the ground. None of the other prisoners so much as moved a hand.

Pitts explained how he had come to be there, the accusation of being "a danger to the safety of America" by a competing minister in Albany who desired his church position. "That is all it takes in New York now, verbal accusations or even unfounded gossip." New Hampshire, he opined, though "not as genteel" as Albany, seemed far more tolerant of diverse political views. "In New York," he said, "they are arresting everyone who has a rational thought, then ship-ping them out to jails as far away as they can—'out of sight, out of mind,' as they say."

Sitting on the cold ground with their backs against the cell wall, Pitts and Joshua discussed the means to survive in Exeter: warm clothes from home, and money to buy food and bribe the guards. "They don't care an ounce if you die here, whether by illness or a slit throat," the minister said. "Money is your lifeline, nothing less."

Joshua could only nod and stare at the other man. The inhu-manity of it all made him mute.

At that moment came a shout from the hallway outside: "Everyone into the yard; it's time for your constitutional. Now!'

Slowly the cell emptied, except for two prone figures who could manage no more than groans. "It's time for the guards to clean and do their weekly count," Pitts said. "Take advantage of it—it's the only fresh air you'll get for a week."

It was a foul winter day, cold, cloudy, spitting sleet and snow. Still, it was a chance for Joshua to have his first real glimpse of the men with whom he shared the dark cell. They were filthy; some looked half-dead—with long, matted hair, dirt-encrusted faces, and clothes that hung off them in shreds. He wondered how many would survive their stay.

"I know what you are thinking, Joshua, but conditions are actually better now, thanks to the good ladies of Exeter," offered the Reverend Mr. Pitts. "Not so many months ago, death and illness were common, even expected. Then, word of the conditions reached the public, and the ladies from the town's churches mounted their campaign. Now we get clothing and medicine, and slightly better food. And they got us this, this enclosure or courtyard, call it what you will. So you see, my friend, how lucky you are to have come here later. It used to be far worse."

Again, all Joshua could do was to stare at his new friend. When he did find his voice, it was to ask the only question that seemed to matter:

"How can I communicate with my wife?"

"For a fee, you can purchase a candle, paper, and writing tools. Mr. Gilman is most conscientious about seeing to our correspondence. Of course, he reads all letters, both sent and received. Be careful what you write."

23

FEBRUARY 1778

SPRING HAD TURNED TO SUMMER, and Joshua had survived. The bright sun and warmth made life at the jail easier, or at least less hard, though Joshua, like all the others, had been fearfully sick at times. In his case, three times: each beginning with a cold, then progressing to a high fever with tremors and near delirium, before abating as suddenly as it had come.

Not everyone was as lucky. The Reverend Mr. Frederick Pitts, as near to a friend as any man there, died an awful, shuddering, week-long death in late April. Joshua's mourning lasted little more than a day. His own survival, he knew, required that he neither grieve nor look backward.

He arrived at summer with a shortness of breath and a constant cough. But worse was the feeling that his body, besieged by a fungus, ringworm, mites, fleas, and lice, was being slowly consumed from feet to scalp.

In late June, with the weather warming daily, he began to hope that the superintendent would allow the prisoners to bathe in the river. He doubted it, though; the guards probably would fear escapes. There had been three already. One guard had lost his job; several others were on notice.

Back in Amherst, Abigail, moved by her husband's description of the conditions, as understated as they were, had mounted a campaign for food and clothes. Just as it was in Exeter, it was the women, mostly, who responded (perhaps, thought Joshua, because up to now no woman had yet been accused of being a "danger to the safety of New Hampshire"). As a result of their efforts, every two months or so a wagon—donated, usually, by Robert Means—arrived at the gates of the prison; for the next several weeks at least, both health and morale would improve.

The weather turned poor again, cold and wet and overcast, in the autumn of 1777. Joshua, who began to feel his health go, wondered if he would survive another winter. He was forty-one already, and had never been strong; a quarter of his cellmates, many of them younger than he, had died the winter before.

That winter, a round of fever left him weak and incapacitated for weeks; he was taken to Superintendent Gilman's quarters, where he was fed tea and kept warm by the fire.

"We have requested wood for the cells," the superintendent told him, "but each time the answer is no. It seems the county officials have more concern for the building catching fire than for the health of you and your friends. Even the ladies of Exeter, this time, could not move them to show compassion in this matter."

That said, Gilman offered Joshua the chance to write a letter to Abigail before returning to his cell. When Joshua, an hour later, handed it to him and, with a guard at each elbow, made his way haltingly back through the damp corridors of the jail, the superintendent sat down and read the letter, then added a page of his own.

Abigail received it a week later. She read it through hungrily, as she always did, then burst into tears, shaking uncontrollably. Her son Charles, across the room, came immediately to her side: "What is it, Mother? Is it Father?"

"Yes, it is. He is all right, I promise. Would you look after the fire for a bit? I must speak with Mr. Means."

Abigail walked, stumbled, and ran the quarter of a mile to the Meanses' home. As Mary Means opened the door, Abigail burst into tears again and fell into her friend's arms.

"Is it Joshua?" asked Mary.

"Yes, but he is all right—so far. I would be grateful if you and Robert would read this letter—I received it just now."

Robert came over to her and ushered Abigail to a sitting room as Mary prepared a pot of tea. His expression remained blank as he read Joshua's letter; then he came to the superintendent's page and fell back heavily in his chair. Still, he said nothing until his wife arrived and the tea was poured. Then, as much to himself as to the ladies, he spoke softly: "Joshua, it seems, has not been altogether honest with us. The conditions he described in his letters were serious enough, but nothing to what this Mr. Gilman maintains."

Abigail began to weep again. Mary Means walked behind Abigail's chair and put an arm around her friend's shoulder.

"We must abide by Mr. Gilman's request that his letter not be aired publicly," said Robert. "It would end his employment, which would be yet another hardship for the prisoners still there. He seems a humane man.

"Mary and I will mount a campaign to persuade the Amherst Committee of Safety to have Joshua brought to the jail here. We'll begin in the morning with a visit to Mr. Wilkins."

Robert, with the help of his wife and Daniel Wilkins, was successful in obtaining letters from nearly thirty Amherst residents, most of them women; the men still feared they would be tarred as Loyalists for trying to aid Joshua's cause. Not that their concerns were unfounded; there wasn't a citizen of Amherst who hadn't heard of the jailing of Joseph Kimball of Henniker, based solely on the report of a single overheard remark.

Six of the thirty, including the minister, volunteered to accompany Robert Means to his meeting with the committee. "Thank the

Lord, Daniel Campbell is no longer a member of the committee," Wilkins remarked to Robert on the walk over. "His hatred of Joshua will not die."

All five committee members, as it turned out, were present. They listened politely to Robert's presentation, with no gestures or expressions other than a nod or occasional shake of the head. Then the chairman, Josiah Crosby, turned to face the group as a whole: "What proof of the prison conditions and Mr. Atherton's health have you?" he asked.

"I have heard of the conditions in my travels to the coast," Robert answered.

"But have you any firsthand knowledge?"

Robert, wanting to keep Mr. Gilman's letter confidential, responded that he did not.

"I am sorry, Mr. Means," Crosby said. "Too much harm has been done already, too many times in the past, by various Committees of Safety that have acted on rumor, grudge, even whim. Provide us with substance and we will act. For the moment, we will let the matter rest, without a decision, so as not to prejudice your request."

Late that evening, over a pot of tea in the Atherton kitchen, Robert reported the results to Abigail, casting them in the best light he could manage. The truth was, he was far from sanguine over his friend's prospects.

The next morning, still feeling vaguely depressed behind the counter in his store, Robert looked up at the sound of the front door opening. There was a face he had not seen in over a year, and had not expected to see—that of Thompson Maxwell, looking a shade older and more grizzled than he recalled.

"I hope I'm not intruding, Mr. Means. I wanted to say good-bye, and to thank you for your help."

Robert jumped from his chair and came around the counter, his hand extended to his friend: "It's a delight to see you," he said. "And in good health, I trust. But what's this about your leaving us?"

The other man explained that he didn't expect to be back to his business interests, or to his farm, until sometime after the war. The more he'd thought about it, he told Robert, the more he knew that his love of the military life was unkind to his wife. "Caring for the farm and children has resulted in repeated bouts of poor health," he said. "It is best I move the family back to Massachusetts to be closer to our relatives. I also made a promise to my brother-in-law's widow and son." He told Robert then of Jonathan's death, and of the promise he had made.

Robert motioned to one of his clerks to mind the shop. Together, the two men walked slowly from the store and across the yard to Robert's house. Thompson Maxwell spoke with animation of the recent battles in New York at Bennington and Saratoga, and of the "glorious surrender" of General Burgoyne in October. "Robert," he exulted, you may be assured of it. The tide has turned. After our many lost battles the past two years, our win in Saratoga, it is said, will bring the French into the war. Final victory is in sight."

Once back at the house, Robert and Mary, for nearly an hour, listened to Thompson's news and to his many thoughts on the progress of the war. Then it was Robert's turn. He related the juiciest nuggets of local gossip, the political happenings, finally the plight of Joshua Atherton.

"I'm sorry to hear of that," Thompson said gravely, shaking his head. "Men with education, such as Mr. Atherton, will be sorely needed in the days ahead. I did not hold with many of Mr. Atherton's views, although in the past two years I have come to understand them better."

Mary, who had not spoken till now, suddenly brightened: "Mr. Maxwell, would you be willing to write a letter expressing those sentiments?"

Robert touched his wife's arm lightly. "Mary, Mary—that may be asking too much of Mr. Maxwell."

Thompson let out a hoot of laughter and gave a wide wave of his arms. "No! No! It is the least I can do, and in any case, I have no fear that anyone will condemn me as a Tory!" He laughed again, louder this time.

"Give me the pen and paper, and I'll write the letter now!"

Thompson began writing. Robert excused himself, explaining that it would be best if the statement were in the form of a sworn document, signed and witnessed—he would see if he could find someone at the meetinghouse or county building to attest to Thompson's oath.

He was gone half an hour. When he returned, Matthew Patten was with him. Patten, now judge of the probate court for the county, was overjoyed to see his old friend. Not only would he witness Thompson's statement, he said, but he would contribute his own as well.

"I know Mr. Gilman," he said. "I have seen the jail. I understand his need for confidentiality. I will incorporate the statements from his letter into my affidavit, avowing that his word is trustworthy, though his identity cannot be disclosed. I am confident the committee will accept that."

Over the next two hours, Matthew Patten completed his affidavit and obtained two more from county officials. He then returned to the Meanses' store, where it was agreed that Robert would send a messenger to Josiah Crosby, briefly describing the new information and requesting that the committee reconvene. All this was done. Within an hour of the messenger's departure, word came back: Crosby and the committee would meet with them at noon the next day.

Mary wanted to take Abigail the news. No, her husband counseled, "no more false hopes. Let us first see if our efforts bear fruit."

He needn't have been so cautious. By one the next afternoon, all four affidavits had been presented—Thompson's, Matthew Patten's, and the two other officials'—and the committee had voted, four to one, to transfer Joshua Atherton to the Amherst jail, but with leave to be absent from actual confinement and live at home until his health improved. Only John Bradford, a close friend of Daniel Campbell, refused the request.

"John, will you agree to abstain rather than oppose?" Josiah Crosby had asked.

"No, damnit, I will not! Outvote me if you will—and I expect you will—but I'll not have this man's treachery on my hands!"

Crosby, it seemed, had prepared the order in advance. All that was required was the signatures from the members. John Bradford signed first, opposing the petition, then stormed from the meeting-house. "Old hatreds die hard," Crosby remarked quietly, then passed the document along for the next man to sign. That done, he turned to Robert: "I'll have this order attested to and sealed by the town clerk; it will be in your hands in two hours. I suggest you give Abigail the news, and make your preparations to travel to Exeter."

By nightfall, Robert had outfitted a wagon with water, two mat-tresses, and an abundance of blankets and waterproof coverings to keep Joshua dry from the snow or rain. He also chose two helpers: the first to drive the wagon, the second to ride ahead and give Mr. Gilman the news of their coming and the substance of the order, that he might prepare the prisoner for release.

They left before dawn, so as to arrive before dark and thereby be able to transfer Joshua in the light. The day was raw, with clouds building; frozen ruts crisscrossed the road. The wagon shook vio-lently, sometimes nearly tipping. Coming back, with Joshua aboard, Robert knew, would be worse.

Mr. Gilman was ready for them. Joshua lay on a bed of straw by the fire, in Gilman's home. As Robert entered, Joshua began to weep and moan; when he tried to speak, it came out more as coughing. Robert knelt beside him. Holding him in his arms, he leaned close to his ear and spoke as gently as he could: "Joshua, it's all right. It's over now. We are taking you home. Only one day more. Be strong."

Joshua tried to nod, but his head collapsed back on the straw. He was in rags, filthy rags. His hair fell below his shoulders and was encrusted with grease, dirt, even live, moving things. The stench he gave off was not just that of filth but of a body decaying. In addition, he was burning with fever.

Robert was now near tears. He felt a hand on his shoulder, then heard Tom Gilman's voice: "He has been delirious for the past week, imploring me to write a letter to his wife, telling her of his love. Until you arrived, he had no hope."

Robert hadn't planned to start back before the next day. But he knew, seeing Joshua's condition, that the trip would take longer than he'd planned. Starting now, he thought, would give them ten miles before dark. They would spend the night in Fremont, at his friend Thomas Beede's farm, then continue on the next day. With luck, they would make Amherst by tomorrow nightfall, with Joshua still alive.

As the wagon pitched and rocked, Robert sat next to Joshua and kept repeating the same things: that his time in jail was over, that he was going home, that Abigail was waiting. He could not be certain that Joshua understood.

They arrived at the farm in the dark. While Thomas Beede tended their horses, his wife, Elizabeth, heated broth over the fire. Then the two men carried Joshua into the kitchen and lowered him into the rocker Elizabeth had brought from another room. Immediately she began the process of feeding him, pausing occasionally to wipe the sweat from his face. Slowly, remarkably—perhaps it was the effect of a woman's voice—he returned to a consciousness, smiling slightly and mumbling incomprehensible sounds. Then, the spoon still in his mouth and the last swallow of broth not yet completed, he fell back in the chair and was asleep.

"Mr. Means," Elizabeth Beede said solemnly, fixing him levelly as she spoke. "I am not certain Mr. Atherton will survive the wagon journey to Amherst. Even if he does, I doubt he will live long."

"I pray you are not correct, Mrs. Beede. But if he is to die, it should be at home with his wife at his side. We will leave before dawn unless the weather worsens greatly."

Abigail could not sleep. She knew it would be hours before her husband could possibly arrive; still, with every crack of a twig she rushed to the bedroom window and peered out. At times her fears were too powerful to contain: She imagined Joshua dead or dying, and would burst suddenly into tears in her bed. It had been nearly a year since she'd wept.

Finally, as the clock in the parlor below struck four in the morning, she knew there would be no chance of sleep. She dressed quickly and descended the stairs to the kitchen. There was work to do, she thought, food, fresh bedding, a fire in the fireplace, whatever could be done to make her husband know he was home.

One by one over the next hour, the children arrived downstairs: Frances, eleven, Charles, four, Abigail, not yet three. Frances was surprised by the morning fire; it was normally her day's first chore. She looked at her mother quizzically.

"Mr. Means has gone to Exeter to bring your father home," said Abigail. "But Father is ill, and we must make ready for him—a warm room, and a bed beside the fire."

Of the three, only Frances had any real memory of their father. He had been gone over a year, an eternity in the younger ones' lives. And even Frances had grown accustomed to the hole his departure had left.

Morning faded into afternoon, then evening, then night. Abigail's emotions swung back and forth: He would be home soon, he had died on the way, he would arrive but die in her arms. She did her best to keep her fears hidden from the children, from the church ladies who came and went with food and comfort, from Mary Means.

Darkness had fallen long before, and still Abigail paced the kitchen.

"It should be any time now, dear." It was Mary Means, who had spent the afternoon and evening here—to wait, to welcome, to console, whatever would be needed. Now she offered to put the children to bed. "You need some time to yourself," she told Abigail.

By ten o'clock Abigail, at last exhausted, was quietly rocking in the kitchen chair and weeping softly. As the clock struck the hour, she heard the creaking of wagon wheels. Even before they had stopped, she was out in the yard in her apron, with only a shawl about her shoulders to protect her from the bitter cold.

"Joshua, Joshua," she cried. And indeed it was he. She leaned over the wagon back, his head now cradled in her hands: "Joshua, Joshua, oh, Joshua."

"Abigail." His voice was weak, weaker than a whisper, his head on Robert Means's lap.

"Abigail."

They carried him into the kitchen. In the light from the fireplace and candles, the sight was too much for his wife. She burst into tears and swayed, moaning, unmindful of herself: "Oh, Joshua, Joshua, what have they done to you? Why did you keep this from me?"

Mary put her arms around Abigail. "We must get some broth into him," she said.

"Yes," Abigail said. "Yes, broth." She bent over her husband, who had been lowered into the chair. Her crying slowed, then halted as she brought the first spoonful to his mouth.

"Joshua, you're home now. You're home. I will take care of you. It is over. You will be well, I promise. You will be well."

AFTERWORD

Joshua Atherton and Thompson Maxwell survived the war, though the men never met again.

THOMPSON MAXWELL

Thompson Maxwell, having played a role in the battles of Bunker Hill, Princeton, Trenton, Saratoga, Bennington, Ticonderoga, and Beamis Heights—not to mention his years of prior service, which included the Amherst militia and the French and Indian War—retired from the military (for the second time) in the fall of 1779, and moved with his wife, Sybel, to his new home in Massachusetts, where he would live, at least officially, for the next twenty-one years.

For a time he tried farming, but it was not a life that could hold him. In 1787 he reenlisted, as a captain in the militia, and served under a General Shepherd in the suppression of Shays's Rebellion.

In 1800 he moved again, this time to Ohio, where he had heard the land was more conducive to farming. Two years later his wife died. In 1807 he remarried, to the widow of a Captain Little of New Jersey. His second wife died in 1813.

In 1812, remarkably, he enlisted once again—at the rank of

major, at the age of seventy years. He was with General Hull's army in Detroit when the misguided and incompetent general surrendered to a vastly inferior British force. Maxwell was taken prisoner. Upon his release from captivity, he returned home only to find that he was falsely accused of advising Hull to surrender. He noted the consequences of the accusation in his journal: "A mob . . . misjudging my patriotic efforts and denouncing all parties concerned in the late disasters at Detroit, rally and gather about my habitation, burn my house, destroy my property, and barely clothed, I escape for my life through a cornfield by night."

In 1814, still a soldier and now seventy-two years old, he was wounded by British cannon at the Battle of Erie, New York; again he was taken prisoner, and again released within months.

Maj. Thompson Maxwell retired from the army permanently in 1819 at the age of seventy-seven. For at least the next fifteen years, he lived—now with his third wife—in the vicinity of Detroit. He died, in his nineties, around 1834.

JOSHUA ATHERTON

Joshua Atherton never fully recovered from his imprisonment; he was chronically ill for nearly the rest of his life. Mostly on account of his poor health, he was permitted to serve out the balance of his incarceration at home, but technically still in the Amherst jail. He benefited from a prison policy known as "leave of the yard," an arrangement that permitted a prisoner to spend the bulk of his time within a specified distance from the actual jail; in Atherton's case the authorized distance allowed him to be on his farm.

His views on the war died hard. It was not until the end of 1778, well after the British surrender at Saratoga and the patriots' alliance with the French, that he officially acknowledged that America was no longer a colony of Great Britain. Having done so, he petitioned the Committee of Safety for his release, pledging his loyalty to the State of New Hampshire and begging its "humanity and justice."

The petition was granted. In January 1779, he took the oath of allegiance to the new government, as well as his attorney's oath. He returned to the practice of law and was readily accepted as a member of the Amherst community. He prospered in his law practice; in one particular Superior Court term, he won every case he tried.

In 1792 he was elected to represent Amherst in both the House of Representatives and the Senate. He chose to serve as senator. The following year, he resigned that office to become attorney general of New Hampshire, a post he held until 1801, when his health failed.

For the last decade of his life, his illnesses were oppressive. On April 3, 1809, he died. He was seventy-three.

THE IRONY

Throughout the war Atherton and Maxwell remained ideological opposites. It would seem ironic, therefore, that both men were later chosen to represent their communities as delegates to their respective state conventions to approve the proposed U.S. Constitution— Atherton from New Hampshire; Maxwell from Massachusetts—and that both voted against the U.S. Constitution for the same reason: that it contained no provision for the abolition of slavery. (No minutes of those conventions were kept, though the speech by Joshua Atherton was printed in the *New Hampshire Statesman* and is the sole remaining record of the New Hampshire Constitutional Convention.) The following is a portion of the speech:

> We do not think ourselves under any obligation to perform works of supererogation in the reformation of mankind; we do not esteem ourselves under any necessity to go to Spain or Italy to suppress the Inquisition of those countries, or of making a journey to the Carolinas to abolish the detestable custom of enslaving the Africans; but, sir, we will not lend the aid of our ratification to this cruel and inhuman merchandise, not for a day. There is a great distinction in not taking part in the most bar-

barous violation of the sacred laws of God and humanity, and our becoming guarantees for its exercise for a term of years. Yes, sir, it is our full purpose to wash our hands clean of it; and however unconcerned spectators we may remain of such predatory infractions of the laws of our nature, however unfeelingly we may subscribe to the ratification of man-stealing, with all its baneful consequences, yet I cannot but believe, in justice to human nature, that if we reverse the consideration, and bring this claimed power somewhat neared to our own doors, we shall form a more equitable opinion of its claim to our ratification.

The Federalists were in favor of the Constitution as it was presented; those in opposition were called Anti-Federalists. The prevailing sentiment in Amherst was Anti-Federalist, and the citizens elected Joshua Atherton to voice their protest. The most notable and influential leaders in the state were Federalists; even so, the ratification was by a narrow margin. The vote was 57 to 47.

Once again Atherton created enemies by his antislavery position. Shortly after the convention, while he was attending court, his two barns were burned. His respect and popularity in Amherst were once again evident by the outpouring of assistance in rebuilding the barns.

ROBERT MEANS

The close bond between Joshua Atherton and Robert Means continued throughout their lives. Joshua's daughter Catherine married Robert Means's son Davis McGregore Means. Robert Means and his sons prospered in the mercantile business; the Means family became one of the most notable and wealthy in New Hampshire. Means served the state both as senator and as member of the Executive Council. Robert Means's home was substantially enlarged and became known as the Means mansion. It was in this house in 1834 that Robert Means's granddaughter Jane Appleton married the future U.S. President Franklin Pierce.

ABIGAIL ATHERTON

In Amherst, more than a third of the men volunteered and absented themselves for one or more enlistment terms, and many, like Thompson Maxwell, for the duration of the war. The unrecognized but true heroes of the Revolution were the women. Their normal work schedule for home and family extended from before dawn to after dark; with the men serving in the army they had the added responsibility of the farm or business.

Abigail Atherton was no exception. She managed the household, farm, and children, Frances, Charles, and Abigail. From the time of Joshua's incarceration in the winter of 1776-1777 until he regained a minimum of his health in 1779, she was the strength of the family. After the war, she and Joshua had four additional children: Rebecca, Nancy, Catherine, and Elizabeth. She predeceased Joshua by eight years, succumbing on October 28, 1801, at the age of fifty-two.

AMHERST

Until well into the nineteenth century, Amherst, as county seat, remained a business, industrial, and transportation hub for inland New Hampshire. After the 1840s, when the county seat was moved to Nashua, the railroad bypassed the Amherst village and industry began departing in favor of river towns like Milford, Manchester, and Nashua, where water could power their mills. The town was now bypassed by politics, traffic, and commerce.

What remained—and remains today—is a small village center, with much of its Colonial and Federal architecture and history still intact. The town common; the Atherton Law Office (where Joshua, and later his son Charles, practiced law); the Means mansion, where Robert Means ran his store; Jones Tavern (the site of Joshua's inquisitions; the Kendall House, where the harvest ball took place); the second meetinghouse (the center of both worship and town government at the time); and the town common (where the Amherst militia drilled)—all these live on, quiet reminders of a rich, important, and tempestuous past.

BIBLIOGRAPHY

Adams, Nathaniel. *Annals of Portsmouth*. Published by the author, 1825.

Atherton, Charles H. *Memoir of the Hon. Joshua Atherton*. Boston: Crosby, Nichols, and Company, 1852.

Atherton, Charles H. *Memoir of Wyseman Claggett*. Concord, New Hampshire, Historical Society Collections, 1870.Vol. 3, pp. 24–39.

Atherton, Charles H. *Oration on the Anniversary of the American Independence, July 4, 1798*. Amherst, N.H.: Samuel Preston, Printer.

A Memorial to the American Patriots Who Fell at the Battle of Bunker Hill. Printed by the City of Boston, 1889.

Buffum, Francis, editor. *New Hampshire and the Federal Constitution*. Published by the State of New Hampshire, Concord, NH, 1940.

Brown, Abram English. *History of the Town of Bedford, Middlesex County, Massachusetts*. Published by the author, 1891.

Brown, Louise K. *A Revolutionary Town*. Bedford, Massachusetts, Historical Society.

Collections of the New Hampshire Historical Society. *Wyseman Claggett,* vol. 3, Concord, N.H., 1832.

Commager, Henry Steele and Morris, Richard, editors. *The Spirit of Seventy-Six.* New York: Harper & Row, 1958.

Daniell, Jere R.. *Colonial New Hampshire.* Milwood, N.Y.: KTO Press, 1981.

Davis, J.G. *Historical Discourse Delivered at Amherst, N.H., on the Hundredth Anniversary* Concord, N.H.: Republican Press Association, 1874.

Farmer, John. *Historical Sketch of Amherst,.* Concord, N.H,: Asa M'Farland, 1837.

Fleming, Thomas J. *Now We Are Enemies* New York: St. Martin's Press, 1960.

French, Allen. *The Day of Concord and Lexington.* Boston: Little, Brown, 1925.

Fischer, Hacket. *Paul Revere's Ride.* New York: Oxford University Press, 1994

Gardner, William M. *Towns Against Tyranny.* County of Hillsborough, N.H, Bicentennial Commission, 1976.

Hammond, Otis Grant. *Tories of New Hampshire in the War of the Revolution.* Boston: Gregg Press, 1972.

Hurd, D. Hamilton. *History of Hillsborough County, New Hampshire.* Philadelphia: J. W. Lewis & CO., 1885.

Langguth, A. J. *Patriots, The Men Who Started the American Revolution* New York: Simon & Schuster, 1988.

Labaree, Benjamin W. *The Fort Belongs to the People.* Manchester, N.H.: The Royal Press, 1975.

Locke, Emma P. Boylston. *Colonial Amherst.* Printed by W.B. & A.B. Rotch, Milford, N.H., 1916.

Leckie, Robert. *George Washington's War.* New York: Harper Collins, Publishers, 1992.

Mc Clintock, John H. *History of New Hampshire.* Boston: Algonquin Press, 1889.

Means, Anne M. *Amherst and Our Family Tree*. Boston: Press of Fleming-Hughes-Rogers, Inc., 1921.

Morison, Elizabeth Forbes and Elting E. *New Hampshire: A Bicentennial History*. New York: W. W. Norton & Company, Inc., 1976.

Parsons, Charles L. *The Capture of Fort William and Mary*. Concord, N.H.: New Hampshire Historical Society, 1974.

Seacomb, Daniel F. *History of the Town of Amherst*. Printed for the Amherst Historical Society, 1883.

Squires, J. Duane, *The Story of New Hampshire,* Princeton, NJ, D. Van Nostrand Company, 1964.

Spear, Eva A. *Colonial Meeting-Houses of New Hampshire*. Published by Eva. A. Speare, Littleton, N.H., 1938.

Siebert, Wilbur H. *The Loyalist Refugees of New Hampshire*. Columbus: The Ohio State University Press, 1916.

Upton, Richard F. *Revolutionary New Hampshire*. New York: Octagon Books, 1936.

Wheildon, William Wilder. *Military Life of Major Thompson Maxwell*. New England Historical and Genealogical Register, October 1891.

About the Author

Robert H. Rowe is a long time resident of Amherst, New Hampshire. He is a former judge and retired attorney. His retirement activities include historical research and being a member of the New Hampshire House of Representatives. He is the author of *Colonial Amherst Village* and *Walking Tour of Amherst Village*. He and his wife Helen live in Jones Tavern, one of the sites described in *Quest for Liberty*.